MW00777813

You Can't Get There
From Here

Books By Megan Gordon

A Month of Sundays: Stories of Love and Loss

You Can't Get There From Here

Stories

Megan Gordon

ALLORA PRESS

ALLORA
PRESS

ISBN: 978-0-9862802-5-2
EBook ISBN: 978-0-9862802-4-5

Editing by: Wayne South Smith, *waynesouthsmith.com*
Cover design by: Megan McCullough, *meganmccullough.com*

Printed in the United States of America

For Mom, you were always my biggest fan
For Heath, I keep trying to change the ending

Contents

Saudade

It is her choice, and yet as he walks away, regret rips through the girl like a knife, imploring her to call him back, but the words refuse to come.

Years from now, in quiet moments, the woman will find herself back in the room with the twin bed, her longing a dull ache in her throat. He will be there, reaching for her, the desire in his eyes reflecting her own. The ache will become unbearable, and while the woman fights back tears, the girl will stand in front of him, naked, pulse quickening, her hands on his chest.

Her Love

Her love smells like lavender. It's the fabric softener she adds to the washing machine when I forget, the scent of her skin when I bury my face between her neck and collarbone, the oil she rubs on my temples when sleep escapes me. It is clean and pure, everything good that I have and that I am is because of it. She tells me I can, and I believe her. She smiles at me and I know I am better than I thought, better with her love. It envelops me when she sits in my lap as we make love, her breasts in my face, her arms around my head, pulling me to her as she comes.

Her laughter smells like red wine, which loosens the knots in her shoulders and softens her eyes. It radiates from her skin as she throws her head back with joy, her face glowing, teeth flashing. She is pretty, but when she laughs she is gorgeous, and in those moments I am full and complete.

Her anger smells like cigarettes, the ones she sneaks when she's had too much to drink, which is more often than not now, the dirty ashtray into which she deposits her self-loathing and guilt. She storms out the door and lights up, chain-smoking until she can bear to look at me again, and the clouds of smoke she blows at me like blame seep into the house through the gap in the back door. The odor clings to her hair, her clothes, her fingertips. It holds space between us until she decides to wash it away.

Her forgiveness smells like lemons. It lingers in the house after an early-morning cleaning binge, and it wafts from the kitchen, the zest in the pancakes she makes for me, both offers of peace. It is the color of her favorite nightgown as she slips back into our bed. It is sunrise, warm and bright, sweet and fresh.

Her betrayal smells like sex. It permeates the place, overwhelming and nauseating, after I've been away all day. It taunts me, winding its way through each room and clinging in my nose for days; I take it with me wherever I go. It sticks to the sheets, mixed with lavender and someone else's sweat. She never washes them afterward; she wants me to know, dares me to acknowledge it. I wait for the smell to fade, I let it overwhelm me and keep me up at night, a condemnation, a punishment for not being enough.

Her contrition smells like industrial carpet and bad coffee. And sometimes a jasmine candle the therapist lights to set the mood. It is artificial and burnt, layered with sensual promise. She is here and I am here, but we are not. She says the right things, but the words have a different sound, foreign and strange, a whole other language. I nod when I think I should and recite my script without knowing what the words mean. We sit in the waiting room, noses buried in paper cups full of bitterness, eyeing each other but not speaking. When we are called she walks ahead of me, leaving sex and lavender in her wake.

Unbecoming

Don't sit like that, they said. It's un-becoming. So you sit like a lady, legs pressed together, twisted around each other, a puzzle lock guarding your precious assets. Later you discover that the tighter you hold your knees together, the more the boys want to coax them apart. If you decline, well, your Saturday nights will be free for the next few years. And if you oblige, you'll have your pick of dates for the prom, but the guy you really like will walk down the aisle with a delicate flower who remained unplucked.

Don't talk too much, they advised. Men like to control the conversation. So you spend too many evenings vacant-eyed, listening to the guy across the table try to impress you with his knowledge of things you care nothing about. He thinks you're wonderful; he bores you to tears. Once in a while you let yourself go and talk about things that light you up inside, but those never get you a second date, so you must choose carefully.

Don't wear that, you're told. It sends the wrong message. So you wear what they tell you even though it feels like you're wearing someone else's clothes, and really, you are because someone else chose them. It's a costume. You're dressed up as a "respectable" woman so you get the job, or the man, or just get left alone. You feel restricted, constricted, heeled.

Don't study that. Don't read that. Don't comment on that. Don't contradict him. Don't be better than him. You exist in the space between expectations and the reality of you, bouncing back and forth with each should, shouldn't, or wouldn't you rather. Instead of the gentle song of your muse, your head is filled with the clattering of outside voices, a cacophony of directions descending on you from all sides.

So you stop. You strip it all off: the dress, the high heels that bind your feet, the weight of others' opinions. You ease into something that suits you. You carry a book with you, put headphones in your ears to drown out the noise of other people, you get comfortable with being alone. You wrap yourself in a cocoon, awaiting your own still, small voice to find you again.

Don't, they say, and one day you put your hands on your hips and say, why not, and they say, it's unbecoming, and you say, I know.

Sense Memory

When I taste salt, I remember kissing your neck when you'd come home from the gym, pumped up, testosterone-fueled, and wanting me, the tang of dried sweat on your skin, the beat of your heart drumming against my lips. I remember how the world melted away, and it was just you and me and us. When I taste salt, I remember loving you more than I loved myself.

That first bitter bite of coffee sends me to the round kitchen table in the apartment we shared where apartment, kitchen, and table were too small for a pair but somehow just right for us. The plans we made on Sunday mornings when the sun streamed in through the window over the sink, bright and filled with possibility. I drink tea now, less assertive on my tongue and reminding me of nothing.

Chocolate-covered strawberries taste like love, marriage, and happily ever after, sweet and smooth and lush. You knew they were my favorite and made up reasons to bring them home to me: Valentine's Day, my birthday, the second Tuesday of March. I bought one the other day and it turned to chalk in my mouth, the richness gone without you.

When I taste macaroni and cheese, I remember standing in your kitchen stirring the roux while you lectured me on the proper ratio of cheese to pasta. When I taste a good one I think of you, soft and strong, gentle and gruff. They brought trays of it that afternoon, gummy and cold and nothing like you. I threw it all away and set about making my own which I left uneaten because, without you, there was no point.

The tang of wine on my tongue used to relax me, but now it tastes like tears and grief and the most profound sadness, an endless freefall into nothingness, where I can't remember you or me or us.

When I taste his lips I struggle to remember what yours tasted like, the softness of them, the pressure. It's fading, though you are always with me in the salty and the sweet and the bitter.

Window

How long do you wait before you know someone's not coming? Fifteen minutes? A half hour? The girl wonders this as she sits on her knees on the couch below her front window, waiting for her date. She also wonders if he'll ever come. She wonders this because she never seems to get the guy in the end.

Boys look at her. Men look at her. She knows this. She can feel their stares while she walks the dog in her neighborhood or buys shampoo at the drugstore. They follow her with their eyes, and sometimes they even follow her home. She'll turn her head and glance over her shoulder as she walks.

I see you.

They don't scare her though she knows they should.

This boy she's waiting for, he makes her stomach flutter. He's cute and sweet and she thinks he likes her too. They're going out in a group, but he's supposed to be her date. Now she's here looking out the window worried that he will never come.

Her mother's friends, grown men, tell her she is pretty. They tell her she will be gorgeous when she's older. She is rangy still, all arms and legs, but her curves are emerging. Other men call to her on the street, whistling and remarking on her ass or her face. She can feel the heat creep up her neck into her cheeks and wishes it would overtake her so she could melt into the sidewalk.

But somehow she is simply not good enough for high school boys. What good enough is, she doesn't know, but she's sure she's missing something that the other girls have. She wonders what the men see that the boys don't and wishes it were the other way around.

He's later still. Forty-five minutes.

He won't come. Of course he won't come; they don't show up when you want them to.

There are boys she is friends with—until they are not. One day they change their minds and they chase away the boys she likes—*I saw her first*—without asking what she wants. She only resists a little because they are her friends. She's supposed to be flattered, grateful even. But when they realize she doesn't like them back, they get angry.

You were nice to me. An accusation. If she is not nice, if she says no—just no—they don't listen. They don't listen until she makes them listen.

Bitch. Crazy bitch.

A truck turns onto her street and her heart leaps, then sinks when it passes her house.

Her first kiss was at eleven, on a school trip. Everyone was watching as Phillip pushed his tongue into her mouth. It should have been sweet and soft and private and years later. She told no one that she hadn't done it before. She pretended to like it, but the only thing she could think about was all the eyes on her. Now she doesn't even really remember the kiss, just the back seat of the bus and feeling exposed.

An hour late now. It is time to give up. She curls herself up into a ball in a corner of the couch and wills herself not to cry. She knows how the other girls feel, the ones with acne-ravaged faces, the overweight ones, the plain ones, the painfully shy ones.

At least you're pretty, they say.

But she doesn't fit in with the pretty, popular girls, the ones the boys fight over. She is neither here nor there, a bit of white space on a colorful canvas.

A boy named Kyle asked her to have sex when they were thirteen. She liked him a lot, but she wasn't ready; he stopped coming around. No one else at school has ever asked her out. There are no Valentines for her, no flowers, no dates for the homecoming dance. Her family teases that she will be sitting on that same couch years from now, alone but for the cat on her lap. She fears they are right.

Fifteen minutes later she hears another truck rumble down the street, but she doesn't move from her corner to look. A horn blasts, and she pops up to see it sitting in her driveway. She grabs her purse and runs out the door.

Obituary

I'm having a bit of trouble writing my obituary. It's not that there's so much to include I can't decide, it's that there is so little that's of any interest. I cannot imagine who'd care.

Someone I used to know died a few weeks ago and when I read the obituary I couldn't help but think that it didn't even remotely resemble her—who she was and what it was like to know her. All I could think was that there should be more. No one asked me for my opinion and it's been a very long time, so maybe the 15 lines represent who she'd become. Certainly the picture they used wasn't someone I knew at all. Maybe she'd changed inside too.

It's been wearing on me for days, the thought that I could cease to exist on this earth and all that would be left would be a weak paragraph that could be about anybody if you simply switched out the names of the people left behind. I imagine some online form with categories like "Survived By" and

"Hobbies." A one-size-fits-all sendoff that feels more like an obligation than a tribute to someone that was loved and will be missed. So I decided that I would write my own and simply add it to my will.

But it's proving to more difficult than I'd imagined.

> Joanie W, (insert age here; please let it be over 100), mother, wife, daughter, sister, friend, left this life on (date of death; any day but Christmas or anyone's birthday). She is survived by her son (name), daughter (name), grandchildren (names), brother (name), and sister (name). She never learned how to knit like her mother wanted her to, but she made that lemon-buttermilk cake that everyone asked her to bring to every single party. She was loved but not admired. Her greatest accomplishment was neither being nor raising a criminal.

Spellbinding.

Except that isn't at all who I am. Or who I think I am. Or who I wanted to be. I wanted more, I know I did. I just didn't know what more was, and I don't think I've ever figured it out.

One of the rotten things about being middle-aged is realizing that you have not accomplished the fabulous things you thought you would.

Never mind that I had no concrete idea of what those things would be—I just figured I'd be successful and didn't worry about the details. Now suddenly I'm in my early 50s and have no idea how I got here. My life is the sum of all the days where things happened that I can no longer remember interspersed with things that I cannot forget. What that amounts to is the part I can't articulate.

Joanie was born on April Fool's Day, a fact not lost on her mother, Anne, who had just started taking the pill when she got pregnant. She'd assumed she was safe to live out her liberated woman fantasies with the first boy she met in college. This was possibly the last moment of being forward-thinking for Anne. When Joanie wanted to change her name at 13 because she thought hers sounded like someone's maiden aunt, Anne talked her out of it because "Nobody is named Taylor."

She was not popular in high school, but she wasn't unpopular either. She landed somewhere in the middle of the pack, pretty enough to have a date almost every Saturday night, but never with the captain of the football team. Although she was a cheerleader, she usually occupied a spot in the back, behind the tanned, leggy blonde girls in the front row. Most of her friends were surprised to see her picture with the other cheerleaders in the yearbook.

I can't work out if it's more what I am than what I'm not, what people will infer from what they read or what is not there.

How do you sum up an ordinary life without making it seem like a cardboard cutout, something flat and stiff?

She was, at turns, a walking encyclopedia, calculator, physician, and executive officer with a ready answer to all her children's questions, the ability to keep a running tab in her head at the grocery store, patch a scraped knee, and guide the ship of her family through times good and bad.

Are our lives simply our relationships to others? Are we significant apart from our friends and family?

I've not cured cancer. I've not brokered a lasting peace between Israel and Palestine. I've not even been able to keep an HOA meeting to a productive hour.

It's been said that what people will remember about you is how you made them feel. This is a double-edged sword, isn't it? Because the longer you know people, the more you love them, the more likely you are to either hurt them or drive them to the brink of insanity. Relationships are deeply personal and staunchly individual; the fingerprints we leave behind on the souls of the people we love are unique, a secret code between two people, one not fully understood by anyone else.

> Her ex-husband once told her she was the most beautiful girl he'd ever seen. He also once asked how she expected him to remain faithful when she looked like an old hag—a few weeks after giving birth, caring for both an infant and a one-year-old—a sentiment he tried to take back after his girl on the side dumped him for someone with more money.

But what if you made them feel nothing special? Would that be worse?

That's where I am. I can't imagine that anyone's day would be different without me. My kids are grown, I'm not dating anyone, my friends have families of their own to fuss over. If I slipped away in the middle of the night, how long would it take for anyone to notice I was gone? And then how long would it take for them to slide back into the flow of their lives as if I'd never been there?

What a ridiculous existential crisis this is. I'll be dead. Who cares? But maybe it's the realization that I have contributed little here and don't have enough time to change it. Or maybe I do and just don't have the energy to bother.

Joanie had a wicked sense of humor. She could laugh at anything and usually did, regardless of whether or not she should. Giggling at a funeral? Check. Her own mother's; she was exhausted. Going to antique shops and finding weird vessels to give to her children to put her ashes in? Check. Saying "Oh, that's awful!" while trying not to pee in her pants because she was laughing so hard? Check. Wait 'til you see the plans for her memorial.

It's possible that I'm not the right person to craft my own obituary. It's impossible to see ourselves clearly. Impossible to see what others see—and they will each see something different. But it feels wrong to leave the fate of my legacy in untested hands. What if I annoyed my daughter the day before? What if my son was tired of me calling him so often? Or I'd forgotten to return Mary's air fryer after trying it out? Can I trust these people to set aside their anger and annoyance and write something fair and accurate?

Hell no.

Perhaps a professional? There has to be a freelance copywriter around who needs a couple of bucks. But will it end up as flat and uninspired as one written by the funeral director after the requisite form has been filled out?

She never really looked her age—except in the morning, when she looked older. Her secret, she said, was avoiding the sun. And a little cosmetic work that no one was supposed to know about. Nothing drastic, mind you, but it wasn't all luck and good moisturizer. Sad though that she felt her looks were all she had to offer and so had to be protected at all costs. If she wasn't attracting male attention or making her friends jealous, what was she even here for?

I've done good in my life, I have, but who remembers those things? Small kindnesses often go unnoticed, overshadowed by other's grand gestures or our own fuckups. And unless the scale of your good deeds was global, who really cares? Have you really changed anything? I am but a grain of sand in a vast desert.

Joanie spent numerous hours quietly packing boxes at the local food bank and once paid for a week at a hotel for a woman and her two children who'd been living in their car. She kept cash in an old travel cup to hand out to folks who stood by the side of the road with handmade signs. No one ever had to ask her for help. She gave it freely, lovingly, and exactly when it was needed.

Who are obituaries for anyway? The dead don't know the difference, and the living will remember the dearly—or not so dearly—departed their own way, so who are we writing for? Are we just putting it out there?

In lieu of flowers, please send a generous donation—we know how much flowers cost these days—to one of the following causes: cancer research, social/racial justice, reproductive justice, LGBQTIA causes, disability advocacy, mental health causes, women's shelters, hospice, animal rescues, or a damn good bottle of wine to share with friends.

Sixty-Seven Miles Outside Jackson, Mississippi

She stands in the backyard of her parents' house. Her house now, she supposes, but she still thinks of it as theirs. She is watching the traffic on Interstate 49, people speeding on their way somewhere else. Who builds a house along a highway? But it seemed to be what folks did around here, the middle of nowhere special.

"Celia, go where the wind takes you," her grandmother used to say.

Celia would visit Granny Albert twice a week at the home. Sometimes she'd be present, sharp as a tack, knowing who and where she was. Other times she'd be gone, living in the little house on the wooded street in Seminary that she'd shared with Grandpa Albert when he was alive, and the only person she recognized was her granddaughter, although she thought the girl was her sister, after whom Celia was named.

But no matter where her mind was, she always said the same thing. "Go where the wind takes you."

It hadn't blown Celia far.

The wind shifts and blows her hair in her face. She's let it go grey and still wears it fashionably long despite the church ladies clucking their tongues at her on Sunday morning. Her first grandchild will be born soon and she can't decide if she wants to look like a grandmother or not. Celia doesn't feel old like Granny Albert looked back when Celia was just a little girl—there were no lines crisscrossing her face, no hoods forming over her eyes. Granny wouldn't have been much older than Celia was right now. But Celia hadn't spent her life working on the farm. Granny wore her experience on her face. Celia did too, but most of her experience had come from books. It was only now that she'd stand outside with her face to the sun.

Growing up, her people had what they needed but not much of what they wanted. And she might have expected her life to be more of the same, existing day to day—work, eat, sleep, repeat—but books took her places. Books were Celia's wind.

"I am going to go to Morocco," she told her mama one summer evening. Celia was just five and had already outgrown picture books. She sat at the kitchen table with the Encyclopedia Britannica, Volume M-N open before her. The glossy pictures of the marketplaces crowded with rugs, food, and people lit up her eyes. It was colorful and busy and alive.

"Why would you want to go there, Celia?" asked Mama as she peered over her daughter's shoulder. "It's crowded and dirty, and they don't look like nice people." She returned to chopping onions. "It's too dangerous. Better to stay close to home."

Celia carefully slid a paper clip on the page so she could look at it later, took the book back to the living room and placed it in its spot on the shelf between K-L and O-P, then walked out the back door and into the yard. On the back porch she watched the cars go by, wondering where they were headed and what they'd see when they got there, until the sun began to set and Mama called her in for supper.

The wind quiets, and Celia settles in the old wooden swing that hangs from the giant oak tree.

Grandpa Albert carved it out of maple when Celia's mother was a little girl. The seat has been worn smooth and bears a slight depression in the middle from years of joyful use. Celia begins to swing. The now-familiar weight lifts from her chest as she climbs higher and higher. Long ago someone would come along about this time and tell her to stop, to slow down before she hurt herself. At the top of the arc she can see for miles; if she can get higher she can see more. The tree branch groans with the weight of her and the motion of the swing.

It might break, she thinks idly. *And I might fall to the ground.* She swings higher.

Celia was sixteen the first time a boy persuaded her to let him take her panties off. They were pale pink and had roses on them. The boy, whose name she's forgotten, was a year older than her. All the girls swooned over him. To Celia, he was just a boy like any other. He'd taken her to the drive-in and started kissing her neck as soon as the movie lit up the screen. It was Benji. Most of the first half of the film was spent dodging his hands and mouth, finally giving in because she wanted it to be done. She wanted to know what happened to the little dog. It was quick, like her friends had told her it would be.

Thunder rumbles off in the distance. A storm is coming. Her feet are back on the ground, her dress blowing around her bare legs. Silver hair flies out behind her. There is more urgency in the wind's song now. Celia feels it push her away from the house, toward the highway. Only a chain-link fence separates her from the speeding cars.

It would be so easy.

A few steps more, then she stops. The wind slows and shifts direction. She grips the fence and waits to see where it takes her next.

The second time a boy got her to remove her underwear she was eighteen. He was a recent MSU graduate on his way to his new life somewhere outside of Mississippi. Carter smelled like Ivory soap and Old Spice, a combination she still found irresistible. He was tall and muscular with a lazy smile and beautiful hands.

"You are so pretty," he told her. "I'll take you far away from here."

He didn't have to ask her twice.

A month later, he was long gone and she was pregnant. Her parents wanted to send her away to have the baby so the shame wouldn't burrow its way into their lives.

Or if not, maybe you could...?

She'd decided that if she went away she was never coming back. She'd keep the child but cut her family from her heart the way they really wanted her to cut the baby from her womb.

"Abortion should be illegal," her mother often said. Until it was her child that got knocked up.

A large gust pushes the round table in the middle of the yard on its side and upends the chairs surrounding it. The wind is getting stronger, pushing the storm closer yet.

It'll rain after a while. But I don't care. So much of what I am supposed to care about doesn't seem very important, and what is essential to me, they pretend not to understand. The red wolf is almost gone from the earth, people are starving in Somalia, and the man down the street beats his wife, but my hair might get wet.

You can't save the world Celia, whispers the wind.

I can't save myself either.

At church, she and her baby girl sat in the front pew so that everyone could stare at her without turning in their seats. Her parents went to a different church, driving thirty minutes just to avoid the eyes on the backs of their heads and the running mouths that wouldn't melt butter but didn't hesitate to form themselves around a good piece of gossip.

Mr. McCready gave her a job at his general store and let her bring Charlotte to work with her. Samson McCready was old and cranky and not well liked, but he was respected. And his store was the only one for miles.

"I ain't doing this for you," he'd told her. "I jus' like making them phonies squirm."

Celia liked making them squirm too.

With eyes closed, she listens, nods, then turns and walks to the porch. Perched on the top step, she takes off her sandals, puts her elbows on her knees, and cradles her chin in her hands. The sky is nearly black, the wind stronger. She nods again; she is right where she is supposed to be.

Fat drops of rain begin to fall on the table and chairs, making loud plunks as they hit the rusted metal. There are several beats between each smack. The gaps begin to close, first slowly, then faster, then with a rumble of thunder, there is no sound but the rain. Celia can't see the lawn furniture, but she notices flashing lights on the highway as cars pull over to wait out the deluge.

Men drifted in and out of Celia's life, some staying for a year or two, others for a week or two. It was she who usually insisted that it was time to go; most of the men that came her way were more interested in a meal ticket than a relationship. When Mr. McCready died, he left the store to her. He'd taught her well, and the business thrived. The smell of a steady income drew men like dogs to their master; they'd flip over on their backs for a scratch, then lay around on the couch and wait for their next feeding. But Celia liked men, the feel of them on top of her and inside her, the warmth and the smell of them, so she'd indulge them for a while—a couple long enough to give her two more babies, first Libby, then Colton.

The rain ends abruptly, the dark clouds scuttling away. The sun peeks out again. The rain has left the air saturated and heavy.

Oppressive. That's the word. An apt description of my present.

The wind has settled, and she wonders if it will return. Without her guide, she is stuck on the porch, waiting for a sign to tell her what's next.

The memory lapses started a year or so ago. First it was little things, like forgetting the word for "stove" or those things on her feet. Shoes. And then one day she looked at a calendar and realized that Charlotte's birthday was three days ago, and she hadn't even called her first born.

"You've been tired, Momma," was all Charlotte said when her mother begged her forgiveness.

"But I'm not," Celia insisted.

"You're fine."

But she wasn't. Sometimes Celia would be startled by the number of notes scattered around her house.

Turn off the stove.

Remember to pay the bills.

Take a shower.

There were times when she couldn't remember the past several days, even though they'd been full of

49

activity. She still ran the store, training Libby to take her place. On a good day Celia was confident that her younger daughter could handle the business on her own; on a bad day she couldn't stand to have the girl touching her things. With a note in her pocket to remind her—Libby can handle it—she wore a red hair elastic on her wrist which she popped when she was stressed to prompt her to check her pocket.

The wind remains still, and Celia remains on the porch. The sun is hanging low in the sky, fighting the dawdling clouds and cloaking everything in an orange haze. Traffic has picked up on the highway as people find their way home from work. She envisions cozy kitchens where families sit around the table passing plates and sharing stories about their days. She envisions herself at the end of most days coming home to an empty house full of old memories she can't forget and new ones she can't remember.

One man had proposed to Celia back when she was still relatively young but her kids were no longer babies. Owen Wright did not spend time on her couch unless she was there with him; he was employed and had his own money and two kids just a bit older than hers. Owen made Celia feel good both in bed and out. On paper they were perfect, but that wasn't real life, and the minute the words came out of his mouth she felt her heart beat so fast she thought she was going to die right there and not of happiness. She was a cornered opossum, and Owen's proposal was a broom about to come down on her head.

"I don't need taking care of," she snapped as she backed away from him.

"I don't want to take care of you, darlin', I want to marry you," he said in a calm voice. Of all the men she'd been with, Owen was the only one who really understood her. "And you can take care of me." He smiled and winked.

"I don't want to take care of you either," she said, smiling in spite of herself.

"Well then, we'll just take care of our own selves." He tried to gather her in his arms but she squirmed away.

"Why do you want to get married and ruin everything? Aren't you happy?" She went to the refrigerator and grabbed two beers, opened them, and handed one to Owen.

He took a long pull on the beer before he answered. "I just love ya, Celia, and that's what you do when you are in love. You get married."

Owen persisted, and Celia relented. They got engaged. On their wedding day Celia woke up covered in hives which grew worse as the ceremony grew closer. A half an hour before the appointed time, she grabbed her intended and pulled him into the dressing room.

"I can't do it," she said, crying. "Look at me."

"Celia..." he pleaded.

"I can't. I do love you."

"I know."

"I'm sorry."

"I know."

They skipped the ceremony, but the reception went on as scheduled. By the time she stood in front of friends and family and broke the news, the hives were gone. Six months later, so was Owen.

All that remains of the wind is a faint breeze, which is only a whisper in Celia's ear. Still, it's enough. She stands up and walks back across the yard, past the swing, past the battered table, toward the highway. Water drips down her wrists as she grips the fence and takes a deep breath. One step, two steps, three steps, and the top of the fence is ankle height. She is ten feet tall. The cars continue to pass by, day is quickly turning to night.

This will be easy. Better for everyone.

Her arms are spread out as if to embrace the traffic, the darkness, the fall. The breeze strengthens, and Celia closes her eyes and leans forward.

The phone in her pocket rings three times before she rescues it and presses "accept."

"Hello?" she says.

"Momma, it's Charlotte."

Celia's shoulders sag. "Hello, baby," she says as she inches down and makes her way back to the porch. "What's up?"

"I wanted to call to check on you and see what you were up to."

A wan smile crosses her face as she looks back toward the fence. "Just going where the wind takes me."

You Can't Get There From Here

You look out the window to the ground below, a patchwork of neat green rectangles with houses that look like they came from a Monopoly box. Homes. You eye them absently and think it would be nice to have a home.

You suppose that, depending on your perspective, you did have one a few short hours ago. But, you reason, that was just a house. A space you occupied with a family you created but never seemed to fit into. They will be better off without you.

"What can I get for you?" asks the flight attendant, a faded blonde woman who probably once dreamed of wearing that uniform and jetting around the world but now spends eight hours a day going back and forth between Atlanta and Cleveland, serving Coke in tiny cups to business travelers who wonder why in the world anyone would voluntarily go to Cleveland.

You decline the offer of a beverage and put your head against the window. You are voluntarily going to Cleveland, at least in theory. Just hours ago you climbed in a cab that would take you to the airport, where you vowed to take the very next domestic flight available.

"Cleveland," the overly cheerful ticket agent had offered, "by way of Atlanta? No, there are no non-stops available to Cleveland. Not from here."

You paid cash. You brought no luggage, just your favorite hobo bag and an extra pair of underwear. A new life will require new accoutrements.

It's your own fault, you understand, that this life didn't work out the way you wanted it to. You had such plans, dreams for the future. You laid on your back in the yard, hands cradling your head, and told the stars you'd see them up close soon. You stood in front of the mirror, accepting your Academy Award as the director of the latest blockbuster. You practiced your acceptance speech for your Nobel Prize in medicine.

"Be practical," your father said.

You saw your future self as strong, independent. You would adopt needy children and raise them on your own.

"Don't you want to be married?" your mother asked.

They told you often, without ever saying it, that perhaps you were not good enough. Not a good enough student, not a hard enough worker, probably not pretty enough, either.

"Mary Jones down the street is so smart," they would remark.

"Mr. Pliner's daughter is such a beauty," you'd hear once in a while.

You took their lack of praise for you to mean that they saw nothing worthy in you, and you could feel their disappointment waft off their skin like drugstore cologne, sharp and cloying. It settled into your chest, became an essential part of you, and all you wanted was to be something, anything but ordinary.

Then David entered your life, and he fell in love with you. Handsome, ambitious David, with his curly brown hair and warm brown eyes. A man like him looked at you as if you were something special, told you were beautiful and smart, and you wanted to believe him so you disappeared into the life he imagined for himself. You painted his dreams over yours and the next thing you knew there were babies and a dog and a pool in the backyard and you didn't know who you were, just that you were ordinary, not the shiny, beautiful unicorn you'd wanted to be but a worn-out brood mare with stretch marks and saggy tits.

So you began desperately searching for the person you were meant to be. You went back to school to earn your master's, but there was barely time to attend class between soccer practices and piano lessons and room mother duties, let alone time to work on your thesis. You joined a book club but quit after the second bodice-ripping period romance.

The affair brought you closest to the real you. He was a stay-at-home dad who'd decided that raising his twin daughters would be more fulfilling than designing houses for people who had more money than taste or common sense. His wife was a prominent attorney whom he was afraid to leave because she would destroy him in the divorce. He knew this because she'd told him so after his first affair.

He'd made you feel smart, asked your opinion on things and actually listened when you answered. With him you were seen, heard—you were there. Somehow you'd forgotten that in the beginning David told you were smart and talented and beautiful, but you never believed him. You never quite understood what he saw in you no matter how many times he tried to explain it. Attraction is about subtleties, things that dance out of our grasp when we try to put words to them, and propping up someone's ego is exhausting, so eventually he stopped trying, which only confirmed what you'd suspected. How do you continue to love someone who doesn't love themselves? The attention of another man while you were searching for the real you made you feel worthy, but the deception was too much, it pulled you away from who you had decided to be. The you in your head was virtuous, above reproach, not someone who snuck around and quietly fucked someone else's husband in various bathrooms around the neighborhood during PTA committee meetings.

You look out the window again, but there is nothing to see, just miles of blue sky. You are suspended in midair. That seems about right. You pull down the shade because you can't keep staring your emptiness in the face. The woman in the middle seat gives you a sour look, so you push it back up. But you still don't want it up, so you put it back down and close your eyes, pretending to sleep so you don't have to see the expression you know she's making.

Behind your eyelids the movie of your life flickers. The sorority you rushed but weren't invited to join. The PR internship you loved but couldn't turn into a job. The birth of each of your daughters, eager, fat babies, one who rarely cried, one who rarely stopped. First steps, first periods, first dates. Now waking up to their first hours without a mother. You left them notes, scratched out on the kitchen counter by the light of the range hood, but a sheet of weighty paper embossed with your initials is a poor substitute for a mom. But then you are a poor substitute for a mom. The words you wrote are far better than any you would have said to them, the comfort more sincere than any you would have given them after a heart-wrenching breakup or the receipt of a thin envelope from the college she'd had her heart set on since she was six. Your wholehearted absence is far better than your half-hearted presence, of this you are certain.

And what about David? It occurs to you that he might miss you, once he notices that you are gone. Yes, you left him a note, but you, maybe subconsciously, placed it in the kitchen, a place he rarely goes. He'll get hungry eventually and wander in there, you think. Any time before that happens, you can't be sure whether or not he'll notice your absence. These days he barely notices your presence. That, too, is your fault. Your bigger-than-life husband deflated when you finally admitted your adultery. He'd suspected, maybe noticing a patch of razor burn on your neck or catching the faint scent of unfamiliar cologne on your clothes. You'd suspected he'd suspected, catching a glance at you held longer than it should have been, an awkward question about what you did one day, but because he never said anything to you, you'd assumed he couldn't have cared less. But you were careless and after a while it became so obvious that there wasn't anyone in your life who hadn't guessed what you were up to. David realized everyone thought him a fool; he had no choice but to ask you flat out. To your credit, you didn't lie. You didn't even hesitate. Of course you were under the impression that it was of no consequence, so there was nothing to lose from your honesty. Until there was. Once your words hit his ears and their meaning registered in his brain, the man you'd spent every day of your life with for the past 20 years didn't look like himself anymore. Your betrayal and the casual way you seemed to regard it extracted something vital from him, tamped down the light in his eyes.

The word divorce never crossed his lips.

Marriage counseling, he'd said, was the way forward. He still loved you, he'd said. We can save this, he'd said.

You nodded mutely, wondering if that were true. It took only minutes for you to know, in the depths of your soul, that it was not true. Not at all.

But you faked it, as much as you were able to, until you knew you couldn't walk into that dull, brown room with the comfortable leather chairs and the box of tissues on the coffee table next to the statue of some long-forgotten fertility goddess and pretend you wanted what your husband did. You couldn't look at the counselor—a sweet, shy woman who always seemed startled when you spoke—and say what you knew you were supposed to say, what she wanted you to say and what David needed you to say. Last week's session was your last, you'd decided. But you didn't know you were going to leave your life until early this morning.

It was some sort of dream; you can't remember exactly what it was about, but when you woke from it, sweaty and short of breath, heart pounding as if it meant to break free, something fundamental had changed. All you could remember was how you felt, like you were choking, and no one noticed or perhaps they simply didn't care. You knew, for sure this time, that you were alone.

So now you are here, thousands of feet above the ground, hurtling toward northern Ohio and a fresh start.

Except.

Except that you are still you, with all your deficits and defects, the same person who just yesterday spent an afternoon wandering around the men's department in Bloomingdale's, watching that cute young sales guy in his tailored grey suit. God, he smelled good. He caught you looking at him, and you slid your eyes toward the fitting room, your expression and body language an invitation. He gave a half smile and went off to help an unenthusiastic teenager with an acne-ravaged face choose a suit for "some stupid wedding." You decided that he didn't reject you, he simply hadn't understood. You drove home feeling old, unappealing, and only vaguely guilty. Maybe a little relieved.

There is no reason to believe that anything will change except your location. But maybe that's enough, you think, as the pilot informs you that you are beginning your descent.

Repossession

"Lock up after you leave," she says, holding up the battered leather keychain.

Riley's mother didn't question my request, and now she gives me no instruction as she presses the keys into my palm.

Twenty minutes later I am standing alone in the doorway of the apartment. It looks the same, as if nothing has happened. The books are still arranged by color in the black wall unit—some standing tall, others on their sides—with jewel-toned glass vases filling the gaps between, the small leather catchall on the metal coffee table still cradles the remote controls. A shock of pillows in conflicting patterns stand in a row on the sleek gray sofa, the white faux fox throw she always wraps herself in while watching TV is slung casually over the back. She might, at any moment, brush past me and start peeling off items of clothing like she always did when she got home. Riley would live in an oversized t-shirt and yoga pants if she could. I smile for the first time in days.

Her scent—a mixture of smoky perfume, lavender soap, and almonds—fills the stark white bedroom we have shared more often than not. The space is immaculate, but the bed is unmade because that's the way she likes it.

"I'm only getting back in it later," she would tell me.

It always made my teeth itch, but it was her bed. Her bed, her apartment.

"I like having something that's just mine," she said when I hinted at moving in together. She is the youngest of a big family; this apartment is the first space she doesn't have to share with another human being.

I take off my shoes and get in, pulling up the covers and burying my face in her pillow. Her scent surrounds me. It feels like home. I shut my eyes tight to keep tears from wetting the pillowcase.

When I wake, the room is dark. The sleep that has eluded me, deep and dreamless, visits me here. I always sleep better with Riley.

My hand goes to my pocket, fingering the diamond solitaire ring I'd planned to offer her at dinner on the day she died. It is elegant and beautiful, but not flashy, like Riley herself. I've been carrying it around for two weeks, transferring it from one pair of pants to another. It has become a touchstone, a talisman. She's never seen it, never touched it, but I keep hoping it will help me feel her. Except it only reminds me of what might have been. I need something else. Her. To touch her, to smell her, to taste her. To feel the weight of her in my arms. To hear her deep, earthy laugh.

What have I come for? There isn't a single thing I want. I want it all. All of the missing pieces of her, the nuance that renders each of us unique. I want to extract something from each item in this place, some part of her that would complete the picture of Riley for me, a still life of a woman I loved, as she was right in the moment that I loved her. I want to move in here and not change anything, to preserve all the bits of her, from the dust on the dresser to the tubes of overpriced almond hand cream stashed in every room.

"I have to put lotion on my hands after I wash them or I will go insane," she always said.

But life would have to go on, her smell would fade and then it would just be an apartment full of memories, those we made together and others only these walls were witness to. Sadness has begun to settle into this place already, a fine layer coating the furniture. The air is still and beginning to stale.

I close my eyes and picture Riley and I know what I want: her Harvard t-shirt. Grey, long-sleeved, way too big for her. It was her favorite. She got it on our first weekend away together. We were in Boston, and she'd forgotten her pajamas. I told her if we were doing things right she wouldn't need them, but she was adamant. She dragged me to the bookstore because she specifically wanted one with the Harvard logo on it.

"People will think I went here," she said, laughing. "And I can honestly say that I did."

She never wore it outside.

"People will think I went there," she said when I asked her why she didn't. I was the only one who ever saw it, but every time she wore it, I would ask.

"Did you go to Harvard?"

"I did," she'd say, even after the hundredth time.

There is a caramel-colored Louis Vuitton box that sits on the top shelf of her closet. I've never seen what is inside but I know it's where she kept things from her past she couldn't bear to part with, reminders of events that made Riley, Riley. Things she would no longer be able to tell me as she sat curled on the couch with a glass of red wine while I massaged her feet. She offered up her life in chunks, the big things that shaped her, challenged her, things that changed her path. But it was those smaller details, things that made her cry, things that caused the faraway look that sometimes crossed her face, that she kept close. Now I want what I'd thought I'd have a lifetime to learn.

I pull the box off the shelf. My hand hovers over the top. Should I wait to open it at home, where every inch hasn't been infused with her? A little distance to blunt the stabs of grief that come every time my eye lands on something else in this room? The ever-present book on the nightstand, the stark black and white abstract I'd helped her pick out at some mega store. The fact that I even know the box exists compels me to look. I'd only seen her take it down once. She never said a word to me about it, but I knew it was important by its very existence. This box and its contents do not belong to me, and there might be things inside that I don't want to bring into my life, although at that moment I can't imagine any part of her I don't want to take with me. I draw a deep breath.

Under the thick cardboard lid there are ordinary things: pictures from college, the tassels from her high school and college graduations, the hood from when she received her master's degree. I set those on the bed, looking for something more, something intimate. And there it is, underneath a worn paperback copy of *Fahrenheit 451*, a short stack of letters tucked into a plain envelope. Riley wasn't sentimental, so anything she saved would be important, a reminder of a person or event that changed her. I wonder if the contents of the envelope are too personal, maybe I should leave them—and the whole box—in the closet. But I ache for her, I want to absorb every bit of her, feel what she felt and see with her eyes. I open the envelope and find five letters from her college boyfriend, her first love. She'd told me that he hadn't been particularly effusive, and he didn't have a way with words like I did, so that these missives exist at all is surprising.

They are sparsely worded—*Did you know that I have always loved you? Right from the start I was yours*—awkward—*When I wake up alone...my legs don't know where to go if they're not mixed up with yours*—fumbling their way across the page—*I will always love you; even if we are apart, I will still love you*. They are more real than anything I'd ever written her.

I'd given her letters. About once a month for the year and a half we'd been together. There were poems and the beginnings of songs and declarations of love, but nothing as personal, as real or as raw as his. First love is unlike any love that comes after; it leaves an indelible mark. A wave of jealousy rises up in my chest, but I don't know if I am jealous that she'd kept his letters and not mine, or that he had felt things about Riley that I would never be able to.

I set the letters aside and turn back to the box. A flash of yellow catches my eye, and I smile at the plastic sheet protectors with concert tickets carefully arranged inside. I laugh when I see some of the bands: N'Sync, Backstreet Boys. Her musical taste had come a long way since then. Any day could see her dancing around the living room with Beyoncé one minute, belting out 80s power ballads while she cleaned the bathroom mirror, or lying on the couch lamenting along with Sarah McLachlan. No matter what she was doing, there was music.

"Silence is just too loud for me," she said more than once.

Her phone was filled with everything from Simon and Garfunkel to Nirvana to Tupac. It is one of the little things I'd loved about her. I don't think she owned a complete album, but she might have owned at least one song from every one I could name. Her phone was the singular possession I would have wanted to keep, but it didn't survive the crash either.

A miniature red lacquer box opens to reveal several small pieces of jewelry, nothing of much value to anyone except Riley. But one item strikes me: an anemic, tarnished gold chain that holds an equally tarnished half heart. Who has the other half? Have they kept it all these years too? There are no markings, no engraving—did *he* have it?

She often told me she loved me, but I wondered if she wasn't saying it just because I had, although she said it first. But she didn't seem to need me; she would have been fine alone, which I decided meant she was a little less in love with me than I was with her.

We met via email. She was working as a junior editor at a literary magazine. I submitted what I thought was my best work up until that point, a 10,000-word story about what goes through a man's head during one 24-hour period. The subject line on her rejection read *Yawn*, the body simply her name and contact information. My reply was a question mark. She proceeded to give me the most thorough critique I have ever had, so I asked her out.

While her words intrigued me, it wasn't until I saw her face that I knew. From the moment our eyes met, I was hers. We hogged a table at Starbucks for hours, trying almost all of the different concoctions and creating pompous reviews for them. She told me about her parents' divorce when she was 17 and how her father had evaporated from her life. I told her about my brother's drug addiction and his struggle to stay sober. I felt like I had a beginning and an end that afternoon, that I was fleshed out and real. I wanted to feel that way all the time, so as soon as I stepped onto the sidewalk, I called and asked her for another date. She said yes and met me outside, and we went to dinner. Indian, her favorite. The takeout menu is in the box, next to a program for her high school's production of *Grease*.

A new wave of grief squeezes my heart and I feel like I can't breathe, so I set the box aside for a moment and get up and walk around the apartment, studying the pictures that dot the walls and flat surfaces. As many times as I have been here, I've never noticed whose faces peered at me from around the room: her mom, her best friend, her sister and brother. Her father is missing, but I am not. There is a picture of us she'd taken when she dragged me to Revere Beach on a bitterly cold day. She'd wanted to go because it would be deserted and she'd never seen a deserted beach. I'm not smiling but I don't look unhappy to be there.

The picture goes with the Harvard shirt.

I walk to the kitchen for a glass of water. Standing by the sink, looking through the living room and out to the small patio where we had coffee on Sunday mornings, I am still struck that nothing looks different. But nothing feels the same; the absence of her hovers over everything like smog, dark and heavy. The place seems to be grieving with me.

I wash my glass and set it in the drainer to dry. Her favorite cup, a big insulated one with black and white stripes and a black straw, sits on the corner of the sink, half full of water. That cup was her constant companion, following her around the house as well as out of it. Why hadn't she taken it that morning? I always imagined her neighbors could tell the time when they heard the ice rattling against the plastic as Riley moved to and from work—now I wonder if they've noticed the silence. I wash and dry it, then take it to add to my stash.

The small bathroom sits right outside the bedroom, and I remember how awkward it was to navigate around each other the first few times I slept over. After a while we fell into an intricate, tightly choreographed dance that often ended with me standing in the doorway watching her put on her makeup. I'd bring her coffee and we'd talk about the day ahead. As I look around the room, nothing speaks to me.

It is the smallest gestures that I crave the most. The way she would run her hand through the hair at the nape of my neck when we were waiting in a long line because she knew I would get anxious. How she would surprise me with a favorite snack for no apparent reason. The way she really listened to me when I talked, even when it was about something she had no interest in. And how she remembered the things that were important to me. Those things have gone with her; there is no item that can hold the warmth of her hand on my neck. There is no thing that holds love.

Hanging on the back of the door is a white terry robe she'd stolen from a hotel in New York. Another smile tugs at the corners of my mouth. I'd watched her stuff the thing in her suitcase, and not knowing what to say, said nothing. As I was putting our bags in the trunk of the taxi, she darted back into the lobby telling me that she'd forgotten something. Through the large windows I watched her hand money to the woman who'd just checked us out.

The robe is soft, and I bring it to my face, smelling lavender soap and the tang of lemon from her shampoo. It smells like morning. Face still buried in its folds, I bring the robe into the bedroom and return to the box.

There is an old journal, its hard cover worn shiny from handling. Inside Riley's neat handwriting notes the dates—the first about eight years ago, the last about three. I pause. She was no longer in the habit of setting to paper the details of her life. Why did she stop? Is the reason in here? Inside is a girl that I hadn't known, one who was looking at the world with fresher eyes, who was discovering who she was and falling in love for the first time. I run my finger along the spine, reflecting on the love letters I'd found earlier. Do I want what's waiting inside? Do I want to watch her discover all that joy and pain—with someone else? That intensity of feeling that takes your breath away? A passion she could never have had with me? I fan the pages thinking if they stop on one I'll read it. I get to the last page, on which she'd written: *The End*. I fan them again. This time it stops on October 26, 2013—around the time she broke up with him. The entry goes on for three pages; it must be something important.

After a moment I realize I'm holding my breath.

The first word on the page is I. *I feel...*

This stops me for a moment. *I feel so sad...*

No. I can't. I slam the journal shut and put it back. There is nothing more here for me. I replace everything in the heavy box and put it back on the shelf.

Her half-full bottle of Chanel Mademoiselle is the only other thing that I want. Sprayed on the t-shirt it would mingle with the smell of her skin. If I close my eyes I can imagine her there with me.

Riley is gone. All I have of her are my memories. My chest and throat tighten, pushing tears up into my eyes. My hand goes back into my pocket, sliding the ring off and on my pinky finger. I don't know how long I stand there, looking around at a moment in time that no longer exists—a moment when Riley was alive, rushing out because she was running late, shutting the door behind her.

Turning back to the closet, I retrieve the Vuitton box and set it on the bed. The red jewelry case is heavy in my hand as I extract it. I reach into my pocket for the ring, rubbing the shining stone with my thumb. The tarnished necklace feels weightless as I pull it from its resting place and release the clasp, thread the chain through the ring, then fasten it around my neck.

I close the red box and set it in the larger one, replace the lid and return it to its shelf.

Mother's Day

Sunday, May 10

My mother died today. On Mother's Day. One last giant "fuck you" to me.

If I close my eyes, I can see the two of us, walking to school hand in hand, me in my pink polka-dot dress with ponytails set so high they just reached her bony hip. Happy. It's been a long time. Anyway, she's dead, and I have to deal with it. Myself. My older brother, Bradley, the favorite, is no help. She would never have said as much but, yes, my mother did have a favorite.

My earliest memory of my mother is the time she wet her pants at one of her legendary parties. There were parties almost every Saturday night when I was young, filled with people I would probably find fascinating today but who are just extras in my memory. My parents collected friends the way some people used to collect Hummel figurines, so the parties were big, smoky, and loud way into the night. Mom was always Queen Bee, holding court in her favorite chair, telling outrageous stories about working in the "rag trade" on Seventh Avenue.

This particular night she was wearing a white halter pantsuit with wide legs that made her look like a movie star. Her blonde hair was tied in a sedate knot at the back of her neck, Grace Kelly style. I remember stacks of gold bangles on her arm and giant gold hoops in her ears. As always, she was barefoot, her toenails probably painted a bright red. She was magnificent. She was also drunk, I think, looking back. She was talking with some man when he said something that made her laugh like crazy. She threw her head back and laughed to the ceiling, then bent over and laughed at the floor between her legs. She put up her hand and said, "Stop! Stop!" as she got up from the chair and waddled down the hall with her thighs mashed together. She made it as far as the bathroom door and dropped to the ground, the heel of her foot planted firmly between her legs in a vain attempt to keep the contents of her bladder in. She put her hand over her mouth, humiliated. No one saw her. No one but me. She looked up and there I was, in my bedroom doorway at the end of the hall, wearing my white cotton nightgown with the little pink flowers on it. I couldn't have been more than five or six. She put her finger to her lips; I've kept that little secret ever since.

Brad was with her when she passed, sitting at her bedside, watching her take her last breath. I didn't even know she was sick. When he called this morning he was hysterical and practically incoherent. Somehow I managed to catch the words "mom" and "died." After he hung up I stood in the middle of my living room. Just stood. My feet were stuck in place. And yet the first thing I did was laugh. I laughed because I remembered that it was Mother's Day, and I knew immediately that she had waited for today to take her leave. I laughed so hard I nearly peed my pants. That's what got my feet to move, right into the bathroom. I made it just in time. As I sat on the toilet, I remembered the night of that party. Where had that Mom gone?

Brad is absolutely no help in doing what needs doing right now. Although he's three years older than I am, he's a good ten years behind in common sense and emotional maturity. When I arrived at the condo within an hour of his hysterical phone call, I found him sitting on the couch, face puffy, eyes glassy and red from crying, staring at the television with a bag of barbecue potato chips in his lap and a six pack of beer at his feet. It was hard to get angry with him when I'd almost expected to find him like that, though I'd envisioned Sriracha chips. I asked where our mother was, and he handed me a haphazardly folded sheet of paper that he'd stuffed in his pocket after the paramedics gave it to him.

And now I'm here, waiting on a call back from the funeral home and wondering whether to wash the expensive Parisian sheets she died on or burn them. Seriously. They are the softest sheets I've ever felt. Growing up, I remember her arguing with Dad about spending "good money" on pricey sheets for kids who'd never know the difference; she thought the comfort of the bed was an important part of a good night's sleep, so first-class bedding was always worth the money. I admit I really didn't appreciate them until I was on my own and had no budget for anything better than a bed-in-a-bag from a discount store. The sheets I have now aren't much better. Tossing these would be unthinkable. Unless I can't get the stains out.

Happy Mother's Day, Hazel, and fuck you too.

Monday, May 11

10 a.m.

They've lost my mother. They lost her. I can't fucking believe it. The hospital says it was the funeral home. The funeral home says it was the hospital. I lost my mother, then they lost my mother, so she's not only dead, she's missing. I have no idea what to do. File a missing persons report?

Brad passed out on the couch last night, woke up this morning, and picked up right where he left off. I'm on my own here. It's hard to remember a time when I wasn't. I've never relied on anyone else to take care of me or amuse me, and I've never cared what anyone thought of me. Anyone except my mother.

1 p.m.

The funeral home just called. They found her. She was put in the wrong cooler. I really could have lived without knowing that. I have mixed feelings about her being found. As freaked out as I was, not having a body to deal with was something of a relief. I've heard that dogs go off by themselves to die so that they aren't a burden on their pack. Sounds good to me.

3 p.m.

Brad is asleep on the couch and I am still sitting at the kitchen table, surrounded by spent tissues and wishing this story had a happier ending. I'm embarrassed to admit that I'd always hoped that Hazel and I could find our way back to each other, that I could have been by her side in her last moments, telling her I loved her and actually meaning it.

My life is divided into before and after. Before is when I adored my mother and knew she loved me. Before is when we were a family and did family things, like mystery trips with Mom and Dad holding hands in the front seat of the station wagon, all of us singing and playing "I Spy." We'd end up at the beach or an amusement park or some town we'd never been to. My dad loved to think up adventures for us, and Mom was always game.

After was something else entirely. An English degree from Columbia wasn't enough to impress Hazel; I'd stopped thinking of her as Mom at that point. It also qualified me for nothing. My first job was writing obituaries for a large newspaper. I loved it, loved painting the picture of the person their families wanted them to be: kinder, funnier, wiser. The dead seem to transcend the mistakes they made in life, leaving their flaws and transgressions shut away in the memories of their loved ones. But in my free moments I would write alternative versions, ones that felt more true to life, reading between the lines of what I was given. "Grandpa believed in tradition and self-sufficiency" turned into "Grandpa was distant and stuck in the past." And sometimes I just got creative and made things up. Eventually— inevitably?—one of my "alternate" obits got mixed in with the real ones and went to print. The grieving family of Emerson Joseph Switt III was not amused that I imagined he liked to be spanked while wearing women's panties. Jobs came and went. Executive Assistant. Receptionist. Now I do data entry from home. It's the only job I've been able to keep for several years. Unlike people, numbers and figures are exactly what they appear to be. There's no transla-tion necessary, no emotional undercurrent. Percent-ages don't care if you're friendly or part of the team.

It's been even harder with men. My heart is ir-reparably broken, something foreign to guys my age. Older men get me but are looking for someone eas-ier, and I am not pretty enough for them to over-look that. As long as I keep my expression mild and a smile in my eyes, everything's fine, but as soon as I say something true, they fade away, retreating imper-ceptibly until they just disappear.

I daydream a lot about long summer days when I was a young, running through the sprinklers on the front lawn with all the neighborhood kids, scream-ing and laughing. We always had Popsicles on the front stoop afterward. Red was my favorite because it stained my mouth red like Mom's favorite lipstick. I'd savor it slowly while I picked bits of grass off of my feet and legs, so I could go inside and show her how pretty I looked.

Now there are no moments as joyous as catching the sprinkler's spray at just the right second and hav-ing your mother join you, screaming and laughing as hard as you are.

I had a perfectly wonderful childhood.

And then I turned thirteen.

4:30 p.m.

How do you do a wake? Is it like some perverse birthday party? Brad seems to think it is. Maybe I should just let him do it; he's far better versed in what Hazel wanted than I am. It's entirely possible that she requested a great party in her honor like back when we were kids.

Birthdays were a big deal at our house. We each had two parties: one with the family and one with friends. It meant lots of presents and two cakes. I thought my parents were brilliant. The year I turned thirteen, my family party was the weekend before my actual birthday, and my friends-only party was scheduled for the following Saturday afternoon. My mother had ordered a special cake for me, white cake with fresh strawberries and strawberry icing, because I didn't like regular yellow or chocolate cake like every other kid on the planet. Pink was my absolute favorite color, and I loved all things pink, right down to my food. I was the weirdo who always ate the strawberry third of the Neapolitan ice cream.

My aunt Gin thought it was ridiculous to buy a cake from a bakery and insisted that she would bake something for my family party. My mother relented and on that day Gin made a big show of unveiling what turned out to be a yellow cake with whipped cream icing and sliced strawberries on top. Needless to say I ate none of it. The cake I loved came from a bakery in the next town over, a 20-minute drive each way from our house, but it was important to her and my father that we each get spoiled on our big days.

I haven't had strawberry cake for years.

Tuesday, May 12

10 a.m.

Brad says we need to get everything in the house divided, packed up, and given away. He's already been on the phone with a Realtor about selling the condo. I've never seen him so driven. He's always been what Mom called "hard to motivate," but I'd just decided he was lazy. Getting Hazel's place on the market immediately is suddenly a priority; he's probably broke again.

Brad is what happens when the oldest child defies convention and becomes an underachiever. He started out strong, was a great football player and a decent student. But then he went into free fall, smoking a joint and playing Super Mario Brothers with his friends every afternoon instead of going to practice or doing homework. He graduated, but just barely. He's been doing just enough to get by ever since. I suspect Hazel was giving him money, which pissed me off as I could have used some myself.

1 p.m.

Bracing myself for the onslaught and the inevitable litany of stories celebrating my mother. Some will be the old familiar tales about her from when we were kids, but there will be others I've not heard before, and they'll be funny and offbeat too, but they'll mean nothing to me except that the Hazel I got looked like the old one, and to everyone else she was the same, but to me she was a stranger. I'm going to pinch my leg every time they gush about her and remember the obituaries. We are always the best version of ourselves after we're gone.

5 p.m.

People have been trickling in all afternoon, bringing plates of food and pictures they have of Hazel that we might not have seen. I don't recognize her in the photos. Some are from before she was a mother, others are after she'd stopped being my mother. For me, she'd stopped aging in her late 40's, around the time I stopped trying to have a relationship with her. She'd been just past her 60th birthday when she died. I didn't recognize the older lady in the photos who wore my mother's jewelry and threw her head back when she laughed like my mom had. This woman had a glint in her eyes that was foreign to me, an edge that replaced the warmth I remember from childhood. There were crow's feet and lines around her mouth from thousands of smiles that were never flashed at me, furrows on her brow from expressions of concern for friends and strangers but not her daughter. This was a Hazel I'd never met.

The Hazel I'd come to know, the one who'd haunted the edges of my life for so long, was not this warm and funny woman everyone described. My Hazel was detached. It wasn't that she ignored me. There was a flatness, a coldness in her eyes that told me she was only doing what needed doing; love was not her motivation, obligation was. I could see that clearly even then. For a long time she looked at Brad that way too. But one day I noticed a change. Hazel's affection for her only son blossomed as the roundness of his face gave way to a strong jaw, his chest filled out, and his beard filled in. He'd become a man, one that looked like a clone of our father. I resented my brother, sure that he was taking my share of Mom—as if she now only had so much love to offer. That resentment mellowed over time, but we were never close again.

My brother made himself in charge of the food, of course, and shunted the hand-holding and reminiscing to me even though he'd spent all this time with her and I hadn't. I wanted to be angry with him, as angry as I was with her for dying without even attempting to make amends with me, but I knew this was just how he was coping. I could see the pain and grief tug at the corners of his mouth and eyes when he stared at the TV screen or when he thought no one was looking. He'd not only lost his mother, he'd lost his best friend. They became very close once I'd left. He'd stayed home and got a job. It took him four more years to move out and get a place of his own. There have been moments in the past couple of days when I ached for him—maybe because he looked so much like Dad—followed by moments when I wanted to punch him square in the mouth because he was so detached from what was going on. Underneath that, I resented him for not trying to get Hazel to let me back into her heart.

8 p.m.

The last of the visitors have left. The dishes have been washed and put away, the food wrapped and stored, the house cleaned. Is this the way it's supposed to work? People come over to comfort you in your grief, bring food you need to deal with, eat said food, then leave you to clean up the mess? You've thrown a party without the good time. One or two of Hazel's oldest friends, women I remember from the past, offered to help put everything back in order, but I declined because I didn't have the mental energy to hear them continue to go on about her as if she never put me out of her life.

There were so many stories about my mother. People laughed. I did too, once or twice. But what struck me was that in all of these stories she was almost the mother I remember from when I was a kid. Sure there was an edge; I suppose it was inevitable. But she was there in those tales, still holding court like the Queen Bee she always was.

That person had disappeared for me. For a few years, I tried hard to coax her back with shopping days and museum visits when I'd come home on school break. I'd call her to chat at least once a week, a painful ordeal of small talk and the status of my grades. I ordered flowers on Mother's Day, sent a card, and took her to brunch. She might as well have been my old kindergarten teacher, one part familiar, one part stranger. It seemed pleasant enough, but I could feel that she was eager to get away. I kept trying. I could have her attention for short periods of time, but the softness that was once in her eyes when she looked at me never came back. Eventually I gave up.

I still sent cards on her birthday with handwritten notes and showed up for Thanksgiving and Christmas with the extended family. While everyone else treated me like their flesh and blood, telling old stories about me, about all of us, wrapping me in the warm blanket of belonging and affection, Hazel simply buzzed around like always, regarding me like I was one of her younger sisters' kids running through the house, to be acknowledged but not engaged with.

Yes, I tried to talk to her about it. She would pull me up short, sticking her hand up like a traffic cop—*you're being too sensitive, like always.* Past is past. Clearly this was my fault. Thousands of dollars' worth of therapy assures me it was not. I am conflicted.

10 p.m.

It was my thirteenth birthday. That's when the line was drawn. It was early afternoon. My party with my friends was supposed to start at six. I was in my room, earphones in, Walkman cranked up with the *Footloose* soundtrack my cousin Laura had given me the weekend before. Downstairs, my mom was busy getting things ready, fussing over every detail, as she always did.

Mom didn't have a chance to pick my cake up that morning, and Brad was probably busy getting high in the woods with his friends. So she asked Dad.

I don't remember much about what happened after the police knocked on our door later. I remember my mother falling to the floor. I remember crying. And I remember hearing the cops say the words "accident" and "head on" and "drunk driver" as I stood frozen at the top of the stairs.

That's when my mother changed. The moment she knew that her husband was dead, she stopped being Mom and started simply being Hazel, my mother. After months of grief and depression, she began to put together a new life, but she wasn't the same person she had been. She never made her way back to me. After the accident, her light dimmed. That stupid strawberry cake. If I'd liked chocolate like every other kid in the world, she could have picked it up at the grocery store and Dad never would have been in the car. If I had liked fucking chocolate cake, Dad and Mom would have retired to Florida. I'd taken her husband, the love of her life, her reason for getting up in the morning. How can you forgive someone for that? I've never been able to forgive myself, so how could I expect her to? But I was a child, a child who lost her father; I needed my mother more than ever, but she could not allow me back into her heart.

My therapist suggested that she may not have forgiven herself for waiting to get the cake or just going herself and I was just a constant reminder of her mistake. That may be true, but the outcome is still the same. I lost both my parents that day.

10:30 p.m.

Brad's finished with the last episode of whatever he's been watching. The funeral home called earlier with details on the services, and he and I have to put the eulogy together. He's going to give it. No surprise there. What would I say?

The loss just fundamentally changed my mother's DNA, and it no longer matched up with mine. At least that's how I see it. I wanted a mother I could talk to about why boys didn't like me and why I had trouble making friends. I needed a soft place to land as I was navigating my first years without the safety of my family. But this was not who Hazel was at that point. Before my thirteenth birthday, there were glimpses of how our relationship would have played out if the accident had never happened. She started to talk to me about boys and how she met Daddy and what falling in love felt like.

I grieve for what could have been every day, even now.

I grieve for my mother, for the woman who gave me life and guided me on its path until I was thirteen. Not the woman who withheld the unconditional love and acceptance every child needs to feel secure in themselves and their place in the world.

I don't grieve for Hazel. I've already cycled through this loss time and time again. The reality of her physically being gone pales in comparison to what I've already lost.

You Again, Always

I t's a shame to waste a perfectly good bed," you said, pushing down on the mattress. "We were always good between the sheets."

I'd come to town, not to see you, but to try to find the person I was, to bring myself back to center. My family was gone, but it was still home.

We'd run into each other at a coffee shop that used to be the pizza place we'd go on Friday nights, the one where you could bring your own wine, which you preferred because you said that most restaurants sold what was popular and most people have terrible taste in wine. You favored Barolo. And sausage pizza. As I looked at you that morning I wondered if I still would like what you like because I still liked you.

But I didn't bring you to my room for sex. I brought you there because... because without you my life had been an unfinished circle, an incomplete picture. Because I wanted you alone, where you'd be vulnerable and maybe tell me that you felt incomplete too.

I raised my left eyebrow at you, a look you remembered well. The fire in your eyes dimmed only a little. You always looked at me like that, with a mixture of desire and disbelief, a look that was somehow sexier than the way anyone else had ever looked at me. Your shoes dropped to the floor, and you laid down on your side, facing the middle of the bed. I kicked off my sandals and joined you.

"So how are you, really?" I said, sliding closer to you. I could smell your skin, familiar under a cologne I didn't recognize, and see the faint crinkles that were beginning to form around your eyes.

"I've been better," you began, then sighed. "I'm still recovering from my divorce." Something on the ceiling apparently caught your eye. "I was a shitty husband."

I nodded, not because I believed you but because I believed that you believed it. "What do you mean?" I asked.

"I forgot why I fell in love with her in the first place." You ran your index finger along my cheek.

"But I've never forgotten why I fell in love with you. Why do you think that is?"

I looked into your eyes. There are mysteries between us, things that belie explanation. I think a lot about how we met, and while I get a gesture here, a smile there, I cannot remember the exact moment. It's as if you were just always there. I remember a life without you, before we met, and one after we'd met, but the moment of our meeting eludes me. It was as if you'd just been out of the room and then returned.

I shook my head. "First love," I said. "Or maybe it's just loose ends. We never really had a proper goodbye, did we?"

"That's my fault. I didn't give you that. I couldn't face it, or you." Your fingers plucked at a loose thread on the bedspread.

I took your hand. "It's not your fault. We both did what we needed to do at the time."

You turned on your back and stared again at the ceiling, your hand still in mine. The warmth of your skin is my strongest memory of you. How you would take my hand across the table or press your thigh against me or just hook your pinky around mine, always craving connection. I put my head on the pillow and tried to memorize the new contours of your face.

"I wanted to marry you. Did you know that?" you asked, still not looking at me. "Wanted it all. The house, the kids, a dog. I was planning a big proposal when you told me you were leaving." You sniffed, and I could see tears pooling in your dark brown eyes.

Those eyes. They were the first things I recognized when I saw you sitting in that coffee shop, alone, reading Neil Gaiman's *Fragile Things,* a favorite of ours. I remembered the taper of your fingers, how you'd run them up and down my side in long, slow strokes beginning at my hip and ending just below my breast. That's how I knew you loved me then, the way you looked at me and the way you touched me with such gentleness and reverence. I could feel a lump forming in my throat. I glanced away, swallowing hard, and when I turned back, you were looking right at me as if you'd felt me watching you, and I felt a wave of sadness crash over me. As if you'd known I was there the whole time and were waiting for me to recognize you.

"No, I didn't know that," I said, squeezing your hand and wanting to take you in my arms and kiss the tears away. Instead I rolled on my back and stared at the ceiling with you so you couldn't see my tears. "I wish you'd asked me."

I missed you from the minute we broke up, the second you were out of my sight. Your smell, the way your arms felt around me. I wanted to tell you how much I hurt because you were always the first one I wanted to tell anything.

Turning toward me again, you pulled your hand away and rested your head on it. You looked at me, saying nothing. Your anger and your pain rippled over my skin even though I couldn't see your face. I didn't turn to you.

"Why? You were getting ready to leave me. Why would you have wanted me to ask you?" Your words were knife-sharp, biting into my heart.

I licked my lips, tried to fill my lungs. "I've always wished that you would have fought for me. I know it's wrong, that it's some dumb romantic-comedy nonsense, but I always wondered why you didn't try to win me back." Heat crept up from the base of my throat. I covered my face with my hands.

113

"Why would I do that? You told me what you wanted and it wasn't me. Why the hell would I want someone who'd only have me if I begged?" Your fist pushed into the bed between us.

I faced you again. "I know. It's not rational, and I'd probably have been mortified but... I had regrets."

Your face softened. Your voice did too. "Why didn't you just come back?" you asked, tracing figure eights sideways across my forehead with your thumb. Infinity.

"I told you I wasn't in love with you. Would you have believed me if I said I was wrong? Could you ever have trusted me again?" My thumb moved to my mouth; I'd stopped biting my nails years ago.

"I don't know," you said, taking my hand from my mouth and pressing your lips gently against mine. I didn't kiss you back, but I didn't stop you, so you leaned in again, with more urgency, and this time I did kiss you back for a moment, then pulled away.

"I can't," I stammered, feeling my breath start to shallow. "I want to, but..."

"Why am I here then?" you asked as you moved over me, looking down into my eyes. "What do you want from me?"

I shook my head. It's a different kind of grief, knowing you will never see someone again because they are gone from your life, but they are very much alive. I feel the stab of not having you to tell my stories to, not having you to hold me when I wake up terrified in the middle of the night, of not having you tell me I am beautiful even when I am not. You are a part of me, sometimes I think the best part, the part that's smarter, funnier, and more alive than the rest.

"I don't know," I replied. "Once I got my shit together I looked around and you were gone, and I realized that I didn't want to live without you but that I had no choice because I figured you'd have moved on by then, that you were with someone else and had forgotten all about me. There was nothing for me to come back to, so I didn't."

We looked at each other in silence for a moment before you retreated to your space. I could see our last conversation playing behind your eyes. Me, holding your hand, letting you down gently,

I thought, knowing I had to go and knowing you couldn't and thinking that meant I didn't love you or love you enough. The look on your face is etched into my heart. I see it when I close my eyes at night, lying next to my husband.

It was a long time ago. I was restless, ambitious. I felt like I needed to get on with my life or I'd never make something of myself. You were a little lost, I think, not quite ready to take on the totality of adulthood. You were content right here, safe in your cocoon. Once in a while I dropped hints about leaving, the two of us, but you made it clear that it was not an option for you, that everything you wanted and needed was right here. At the time, that included me. I didn't think that I was special enough to make you leave everything you'd ever known behind.

I tried, I really did. I tried to be here with you, tried to find ways to make my dreams come true without leaving you, but there weren't many options, and eventually my need to leave was overwhelming. I believed that I could go, that we could stay in touch, and that eventually we'd be together again. But when I told you, you asked me how I could leave you, and I thought about it for a moment and told you that I guessed I wasn't in love with you—I loved you, of course, but I wasn't in love.

"I couldn't figure out how to make you understand, so I just said it." I sat up in the bed and pulled my knees to my chest. "I regretted it instantly and probably knew it wasn't true, but it felt a little true. How could I leave you if I really was in love with you?" My hands combed through my hair, pulling at it a bit. "I couldn't imagine my life without you, so I wanted to keep you in it somehow. We could be friends, talk about everything like we always did, get some life experience, then find our way back to each other. But you never called, and when I called you, your number had been disconnected."

You sat up too, legs crossed, facing me. "I couldn't move on as long as there was a connection between us, so I just cut you off. It still took years to get over you. Maybe I never have, I don't know. At some point I decided it was time to have a life, and then I met Patty. I loved her, but she wasn't you. Eventually she realized that she never had all of me and she knew she never would. After the divorce I just resigned myself that there was no happy ending for me without you. I've made peace with it."

I started crying. At first just a few hot tears streaming down my face, but then the chest-heaving sobs started. You took me in your arms and held me while I let out everything I'd been holding onto for years. When I pulled back I saw that you'd been crying too.

You were never shy about showing your feelings; it was one of the things I loved about you the most. You had this gentleness, a sensitivity that is missing in so many men. It took years to find someone who wasn't just a pale shadow of you, someone I could love even if they weren't you.

He is a good man, a good husband, but there has always been this hole inside me that no one else could fill. You have always owned a part of me, and I long ago accepted that, without you, I'd just go on with that piece missing. Life has been good to me, but as I got older, I started to realize how quickly time was slipping away, and that empty space began to feel bigger. I never felt like it was over, not completely. And then out of nowhere I started feeling the loss in a more profound way than I had all those years ago. Some part of me had held out hope that we would be an us again.

"I'm sorry," I said after I'd composed myself. My voice was steady even as tears still etched lines down my cheeks. "I'm sorry that I hurt you, that I ruined us, that I made you unhappy..."

"Hey," you said, lifting my chin with your hand. "You didn't make me unhappy. I made me unhappy because I couldn't be where I was, I couldn't pull myself out of the past. You did what you did to take care of yourself, to get the life you needed. I didn't really believe that you'd leave without me, and I waited for you to ask me to go with you, never realizing I'd already said no over and over."

"So now what?" I asked you. New tears were forming in my eyes as I waited for your answer, as if it was all in your hands, as if only you had the choice.

You shook your head but said nothing. I waited a moment more, never taking my eyes off of yours. There was no good answer, I knew that. So did you. But neither of us were willing or able to form our mouths around the words. If we said it out loud it would be true. There was no happily ever after, no way for everyone to come out of this unbroken. All that was left was a choice, and it was mine.

Fear held my tongue. Fear of letting you walk away from me forever this time, fear of upending my comfortable existence for something untested by time and hardship, fear that my long-running fantasy of us would turn out to be something less than what I was leaving behind, fear that you would ultimately find me to be a disappointment and I would be left alone. I was afraid to choose and afraid not to. Of course, not choosing is a choice, isn't it? You never wavered in choosing me but understood my hesitation as a tacit rejection of you. I couldn't say yes to you even if I couldn't say no.

Fresh tears shone in your eyes as you kissed me again, full of longing and sadness. And I kissed you back, full of regret and guilt. Your hand cupped the side of my face, your thumb following the line of my jaw. I didn't touch you at first, trying to find some higher moral ground by holding back, but the pretense fell away as you began to kiss my neck. My eyes were closed and behind my lids I saw you as you were, us as we were. It was as if no time had passed. My hands found their way under your shirt and up your back, the landscape so familiar I could trace the birthmark under your shoulder blade by memory. Your mouth moved down to the hollow of my throat and my body knew how it was to respond. I tilted back my chin and arched toward you, answering the question your lips asked without a sound. It didn't take long for our clothes to end up in a pile on the floor, and it seemed that this would all be over too quickly but, as you realized it too, you slowed down, mapping the contours of my body with your fingertips, your eyes, your mouth. I buried my face into your neck, taking in your scent, trying to recommit it to memory so I could keep it with me always. Your tears had started again as our bodies came together, but you never took your eyes off of mine. My breath caught, and I wanted to look away, but I couldn't.

I keep no pictures of you, no physical evidence of your existence, but the memory of that day, much fresher than any other, lingers in the space you left. You are the alpha, the source of my love, but I knew when you stood in the doorway and turned to look back at me that we were just moments for each other in this life, that this was the period at the end of our story.

Strange Secrets Worth Knowing

Had he known then what he knew now, the knife would have stayed in the maple block with all the others; the blue tarp spread on the floor would have remained in his garage; and that couple from North Platte, Nebraska would be wandering through this house, opening cabinets and complaining about the seafoam tile in the second bathroom—they all complained about that tile and with good reason. But it was too late for that, and regrets were part of life, weren't they?

It was not as if he hadn't taken time to think this through. These things can't be done willy-nilly. The stakes were too high. This was what he had wanted. Or thought he had wanted. Strange how the reality of a thing can tarnish the glow it had while it only lived inside the mind.

Even several minutes earlier, before it was done, he'd felt such shivers of anticipation that he'd had to remind himself to take his time and do it properly. Delicate business, death.

The house was empty and immaculate, no furniture and not even a scrap of paper left behind. He prided himself on showing homes only in the best possible shape. It's the reason he was the number one agent in two counties. He'd chosen this place because it was empty and because no one had asked to see it in several weeks—until yesterday. Susan and James were moving from Nebraska because they thought they would have a better life here. They needed something inexpensive, and this house fit the bill because it was, basically, a dump. He'd put them off until Saturday, after it was done. Of course they wouldn't be able to see it then either because— well, obviously.

They are better off, he thought.

The house didn't have good light, and it was gloomy and depressing and now it would be really depressing. What this property was good for was razing and building something better. That's why he chose it.

Everything had run according to plan, so why the doubts now? They'd started the minute the blade of the knife had slid through the flesh.

It was a beautiful thing really. He regularly honed and sharpened each of the blades in his kitchen to keep them in top condition and it showed with this slice—he'd barely had to put any pressure on the hilt and it sailed through the skin as if it were soft butter.

The moment was perfect but the doubt flowed with the first strong stream of blood. It did not deter him, and he finished the job. But now? He was wishing it had. Maybe he could have turned it around.

The doubt crept in because the anger had dissipated with the first bite of the knife. He'd counted on the anger to carry him through the whole procedure. Now he tried to call it back up, but he found himself unable to. He couldn't remember not feeling angry somewhere underneath, even when he was happy. It was always there, doing its work even when he didn't think about it, like a gallbladder or kidney. It was wound into his DNA, it lived in his cells and multiplied with them. Except now it was just gone.

He felt the absence of it, a phantom pain deep inside of him.

Or was that regret?

He'd done it, and there was no going back. Ever. There was nothing he could do.

What's done is done, he told himself. *Don't panic. It will only make things worse. Follow your plan.*

He looked at the tarp, which was doing its job nicely. He'd staked up the corners so the sides curved up and caught all the blood. There was so much blood, more than he'd really anticipated, but the tarp held all of it. Later the body could be rolled up in it and that would be that. No cleanup required.

He wished she wouldn't have left him. None of this would be happening if she had just stayed. They were happy together. At least he was happy. The day she left, she told him that she hadn't been happy in years. Years. Why hadn't he noticed? Why hadn't she told him? She should have told him then he could have fixed it and she wouldn't have left. She was the source, the center of his rage. This was her fault. His breathing became ragged and shallow.

Someone would find the body tomorrow, before it started to smell. An associate of his was showing the house to those kids from North Platte. She'd arrive early to make sure everything was in order, and she'd call the police. He'd be long gone. His plan was simple and neat. He'd done well.

Except that now he wished he hadn't been so thorough. Tomorrow was a new day; things could have gotten better, but now they never would.

He was alone. And that, of course, was the heart of it all. He was alone and had been for a very long time. His wife—the source of his passion, the source of his rage—left him many years ago. They'd had no children. She left, and he was alone and alone he stayed and alone he was right now.

Alone and dying.

That he chose to die in one of his houses wouldn't be surprising to people; his work was his life. All of it. It was his livelihood, his passion, and his social world. When did it stop being enough?

He'd been toying with the idea of killing himself for some time, and made this plan a while back but hadn't really been serious about it. Until yesterday. Susan and James appeared in his office around ten yesterday morning. They were impossibly young. Her belly was round, with the navel sticking out like one of those timers they put in chickens that pop up when they're ready. He was tall and skinny with a beard that wouldn't fill out for another couple of years. They were excited, happy. Starting a new life.

All he had was his old one.

The couple's enthusiasm and cheer wore on him, sapping his energy and, apparently, his very will to live. As he pulled up a few listings for them his plan popped into his head.

It's time. It's time for me to go because who gets annoyed and depressed at a cute young couple who are about to have a baby?

He made arrangements with Cindy, his protégé, to show the kids a few places, taking care to add this house to the list. Cindy was young, smart, and capable. She would continue to run the office after he was gone. And she was tough enough to handle finding him lying in a bath of his own blood in the middle of the living room.

A perfect plan, perfectly executed.

Except.

Now he didn't want to die; he forgot why he wanted to in the first place. All that remained were things he hadn't done, the parts of life that he missed. This was not what he had expected; he expected release. The letting go of the pain, the anger, the frustration, the loneliness. He thought it would all drain away along with the platelets and white cells. But it just evaporated, leaving only fear. Or maybe it was just the survival instinct, fighting to live even when we don't want to. He had wanted to die so badly it never occurred to him that he might ever want to live.

God is a son-of-a-bitch. Can't make head or tails of life even at the end.

He'd hoped for clarity but was denied. So he was here, dying, not wanting to die but wanting to want to die.

He could remember how blue the sky was on his wedding day. He could remember the Christmas morning when he was 12 and got the bicycle he was praying for. But he couldn't remember the kick in his gut when his 20-year marriage ended abruptly or his sorrow at his mother's death when he was 18 or how much he missed her at his college graduation.

This must be Hell.

A film of all the best moments in life, taunting him with joy and wonder, leaving out the dark parts, the things that cut him to the bone, what ripped his heart out and left it in the middle of the rug. Things that led him to be lying on the floor in a pool of his own blood, the room getting darker and darker even though it's only two in the afternoon.

And it felt so long. Years, a lifetime. His lifetime, a vast expanse of once-blank slate now packed with chalk marks. Words. Faces. The imprint of his hand. Each moment he experienced there for him to see even as it was erased.

But it is too late to stop it. His phone is still in his car out front, and he is too weak from loss of blood to move. His breathing is growing more shallow and ragged by the moment, and he can feel himself slipping away.

Then the cold comes. It starts from the inside, like a fan blowing on his liver, then kidneys, then upward. By the time it makes it to his skin, he is shaking so hard he fears the blood will splash outside the tarp. He worries that it will stain the wood floor. And then he smiles. Or wants to. Why, now, should he care about the floor in a crappy house that he wouldn't be around to see sold or demolished or turned into a group home that the neighbors would complain about? He wouldn't see Cindy open the front door and find him there, bathing in his own blood.

First she'd curse. "Fuck." Then she'd realize it was him. "Fuck you, Charlie. Fuck you all the way to Hell." This was a terrible thing to leave for someone else, but even if he died naturally someone would have to deal with what was left of him, and who else would even notice he was gone? Cindy. She was in for it either way. She might even shed a tear or two when she found out he'd left her everything. Was she like the daughter he never had? Not even close. But there was no one else, and he knew she'd take care of the one thing that meant anything to him in life: his name, his reputation.

All at once, feeling replaces thinking, emotions called up as sense memories. He smells hot asphalt and night-blooming jasmine; baby powder and White Shoulders perfume; and the base of his ex-wife's throat. He hears her humming as she makes dinner; the way she moans beneath him when they make love; the sound of her laughter. He can see her smiling at him from behind her veil; the leaves on the trees in his front yard turning in the fall; the rise and fall of her chest as she sleeps next to him. There is no physical sensation but cold. No caress of sun on his face; no sweet, tentative pressure of their first kiss; no warmth of her skin on his. And then there is nothing at all. No pain, no joy. Nothing.

Charlie Baker is dead.

The Hole in the Back Fence

There is a hole in the back fence. It's where the dogs get out even though we've covered it again and again.

I made Greg put in a window over the sink so I could see outside, so I could see the spot.

"Maybe I can catch the dogs trying to sneak through," I'd said.

So we knocked a hole in the wall and I watch the dogs wriggle through the fence and wish them luck. They disappear for hours, but they always come back by dinner time.

Until they don't.

After a few days Greg begins to worry about the pups. Maybe they've been hit by a car. Maybe someone has taken them. I nod silently; I'm oddly comforted by the idea that they may be dead because then I don't have to watch them leave while I manage the breakfast dishes, scraping dried egg from the frying pan and wondering where they go and what they do all day while I am stuck here.

My hopes and dreams slipped through a crack in my life and left me a long time ago. I imagine them fleeing, running down the street with the dogs, eyes alight and hearts soaring. Free.

The hole is big enough for me to crawl through. I think about that, squeezing through and disappearing for a few hours, a few days, forever. I think about it a lot when I'm washing dishes. I stare out the window and imagine what I'd do.

A week later, Greg makes posters to put up around the neighborhood, as if our neighbors aren't well acquainted with our shaggy escape artists. They've all brought one or the other home more than once. We've called, and no one has seen them for days. He checks the pound, but they haven't shown up there. *Clever dogs*, I think, eluding capture. I wonder if Greg would put as much effort in looking for me as he is for Dash and Dot. They are his babies—he picked them, named them, nurtured them. We, the three of us, are his whole family.

Before we were married, my world was big and loud, sometimes chaotic. I was in love with a brilliant man with bipolar disorder who wouldn't stay on his meds because they interfered with his creative drive. The uncertainty, the constant turmoil, was maddening. I needed him to lead the way, and the path he was taking was headed into oncoming traffic. And then I met Greg, so calm and centered. I was mesmerized. He made me feel safe and stable. I fell in love. It only took a few years to lull me to into this sleep state, this place where inertia holds my body in place even as my heart is planning my getaway. It's not his fault; it's mine. I let myself drift in Greg's calm waters too long, and I lost my fight, my fire. So secure, so peaceful, so loved—what else did I need?

The dogs have been gone two weeks and my husband is despondent. He's left flyers all over town, talked to anyone who'd listen. There's been no sign of our wayward Goldens. I imagine them living a whole different life with a whole different family, one with kids and noise and mess. A joyous, full life.

I make all the appropriate noises about the dogs. I know he is hurting and I hurt for him, but somewhere deep inside me I think, they chose this. They were willing participants, whatever has happened to them. Perhaps they haven't come home on purpose or maybe they've met with foul play, but they chose to leave the safety of the backyard, the protective cocoon of this existence. Anything worth having involves risk, does it not?

And yet I am not so eager to take that risk, to fly without a parachute, to jump and not look down. Since the dogs have been gone, I think a lot about what I wanted versus what I have and wonder why I cannot be satisfied with a perfectly nice life.

But that's the thing, isn't it? Nice. It's supposed to be positive, but it's a slippery little word, a veneer over the banal and mundane. Nice. Nobody aspires to a nice life unless the one they have is a mess. Those with comforts and privilege don't seek a nice, quiet life; they want to make noise, live large, and leave a mark on the world. Like I did once. I was supposed to be ambitious and accomplish things, like any good daughter of the '80s.

It's been three weeks and still no sign of Dot and Dash. Greg has begun to grieve, a process I can only watch from afar. I wonder if he'd grieve for me that way; I decide he probably would not. Maybe at one time, but not anymore.

When we were first married he would write me notes and leave flowers on my windshield. Sometimes we'd not make it to our dinner reservations because he could not keep his hands off of me. Over time that has ebbed away. I can't remember the last time we made love. Probably before the dogs went missing.

He alone is not to blame. In our early years together I would write notes and slide them into his briefcase, trace "I love you" in steam on the mirror when he showered in the morning, touch him any time he was near me. I can't remember the last time I put my hands on him.

And now we are here, just the two of us. The house has become very quiet. I hadn't realized how much life the dogs brought here, how much we talked to each other through them, or talked about them or to them. The two of us alone didn't seem to have much to say to each other. But he looks so lost and so sad I feel as if I must try to reach him because now I'm all he's got and he's not able to ask for what he needs.

Greg's favorite dinner is chicken pot pie. It reminds him of when he was a kid and his mother used to put two of the frozen ones in the oven for them and the two of them would play cards until dinner was ready. It was just the pair of them then, after his father had left them to start a new family somewhere else. He remembers these as happy times, after the upheaval his father caused in their lives. I want him to be happy again, just for a while at least, so I make him a homemade pot pie. He's excited when I put it in front of him, but I see that light in his eyes dim. It is not the same as the frozen one, which was mostly crust soaking in gravy with a few bits of vegetables and chicken. He doesn't like the addition of green beans either, or the thyme in the seasoning. He finishes it, though, and kisses me on the top of the head before he goes into our bedroom and shuts the door.

I attempt a second connection a few days later. He likes to shower when he comes home from work, to wash off the day. This night I wait a moment after he steps in, then I follow. He seems startled by my presence; he looks at me as if he's never seen me naked before. And perhaps it's been so long that he actually hasn't seen this version of me. I reach out and touch him on the arm, and he pulls me to him. We stand there silently for what seems like hours, just holding each other. There is no kissing, no caressing, no sex. Just contact. And it is enough for now.

"Maybe we should think about adopting another dog," he says to me one Saturday afternoon. The dogs have been gone for over a month now, and we've been inching our way back to each other. We'd made love only that morning.

"I don't know," I say. I'm afraid, actually. I haven't thought about the hole in the fence for over a week. I feel lighter than I can remember feeling in a long time. It's a balance too fragile to risk upsetting.

I see the disappointment on Greg's face. "I'll think about it," I say with a smile. I'm not sure if I mean it or not. I want him to be happy but it suddenly occurs to me that I want him to be happy with me. I want to be enough.

I resisted having children for as long as I felt I could. Greg wanted a family and I wanted Greg, so I stopped taking the pill. Six months in, I lost our daughter, Ashley. I mourned. I blamed myself; I couldn't bear to try again. Greg never blamed me, and I wished he would because it would have been so much easier to be angry with him than angry with myself. But maybe he does blame me? Maybe he lied when he said it was okay, that we'd make our own kind of family. I guess we did; a couple of years ago he came home with two furry little souls with outsize feet and friendly brown eyes. He poured his love into them. Sometimes I felt he gave them my share as well, that he gathered up what he'd felt for me and redirected it. I could never pinpoint it exactly; it was just a feeling. I guess I believed he should mourn along with me, withhold the love he'd have had for our child for some "respectable" period. That he didn't seemed a rejection of me, of the part of our progeny that would have been me. The dogs were not of me, so he was free to put all of his love and care into them instead.

It never occurred to me that all I had to do was reach out and touch my husband, look him in the eye and say, "I miss you. I love you." But I couldn't take the chance that he would reject me. So I kicked a small hole in the fence and let the dogs do the rest. I willed them to run away, to get lost so Greg would find his way back to me on his own.

It's been two months since the Great Escape, and I am washing the breakfast dishes when I see some movement in the backyard out of the corner of my eye. When I look up I see Dot and Dash—dirty, considerably thinner, and looking oddly relieved—slipping in through the hole.

My heart leaps.

Other Men's Sons

He served his country. Fought in Korea and had a chunk of shrapnel still stuck in his right thigh. On Sundays in football season he would rub the raised scar when the Packers needed good luck. His son had asked him why he thought it was lucky.

"It didn't kill me," came the answer.

But Robbie often wondered if it didn't kill something inside his father. There was always something inside Robert, Sr., a small, callous kernel in his heart that made it hard for him to tolerate people who were different.

Robert was all of eighteen when his number came up; he had never even heard of Korea. It took him ten minutes with a world map to find the country he was being sent to. He didn't fully understand what was going on, but he knew that he was going to kill Commies, and that was all he felt he really needed to know. He pointed his rifle where he was told to and killed who he was told to. He never got close enough to look any of them in the eye. He couldn't tell a North Korean from a South Korean from a Chinese from a Japanese. He may have tried once or twice, but eventually he just disliked all of them equally. Let someone else sort them out.

What amazed Robbie was that his mother married his father at all. While Robert was away at work, Mary would sneak the local down-on-their-luck souls into the house, feed them, wash their clothes, and let them take a bath. In return they would fix things around the house. On their way out the door in the afternoon, she'd slip them the money earmarked for the handyman she never hired. Robbie was sworn to secrecy at an early age, although it never would have occurred to him to tell his father. He inherited his soft heart from his mother, and it was that soft heart, Robbie supposed, that enabled her to stay with her husband. Maybe he was a different person when it was just the two of them.

Mary had always been too tall and just missed being beautiful by a few fractions of an inch between her eyes. Robert was different from the other boys she knew. He seemed more worldly and more sophisticated. He seemed to have his life together. And he liked her. But there was something else. He was visibly broken. His face was all angles and planes, devoid of the roundness of youth. His eyes had hardened and his lips had tightened. Mary's heart broke for him when they met. She wanted to fix him, to make him whole again. Take the sadness from his eyes. She soon realized love couldn't bring him all the way back. She married him because back then it was what you did when you got pregnant. Robert gave her Robbie, the love of her life. She never looked back.

Robert was neither cruel nor abusive. He was just... detached. Distant. Rigid. He saw the world as black and white, right or wrong, good or bad, and nothing anyone could say would sway him. Mary saw the world in shades of gray; there was always a middle ground. Over the years she had found that with her husband.

It seemed to Robbie that his father lacked compassion. That had become particularly apparent when the Vietnam War came into their home via the nightly news. Usually his father left the room when the images of young men in uniform came on the screen, leaving Robbie alone to interpret what he was seeing, to make sense of boys, not much older than he was, burning villages and hunting earnestly for "Charlie." Other times Robert stayed, commenting here and there.

"The Commies are like roaches. You smash 'em down, and they just keep coming," he said one evening.

Robbie said nothing. He was conflicted about the war. He didn't share his father's certainty that the American Way was the only way. He wanted to believe in something; he just couldn't land on it.

He watched the footage of men—boys—with dirty faces and helmets on their heads that looked two sizes too big, as if they were playing soldier. Their faces looked so young but their eyes looked so old.

And then there were the draft dodgers.

"They ought to shoot 'em on sight. Cowards."

"Not everyone is able to kill, Dad," said Robbie. "Not everyone is willing to die in someone else's fight."

"You won't think it's someone else's fight when those reds come marching straight down Oak Street.

If we don't keep them in their place, they'll come for us eventually."

There was no point in trying to change his father's mind; Robbie needed to make sense of things on his own. He frequently wandered over to the U W campus in Madison to watch protests and listen to speeches. He was enthralled when protesters gathered 250,000 people for the March Against Death demonstration in Washington DC in November 1969, carrying signs with the names of soldiers who died in Vietnam.

"Amazing," said Robbie, wondering if it would make any difference.

"Ungrateful hippies," said Robert, wondering the same.

The students' passion was intoxicating, but there was often something else that unsettled Robbie. Once he saw a protestor spit on a young man in a wheelchair, yelling, "Baby killer!"

"Do they kill babies?" he asked his father.

"Don't buy in to all that college propaganda. Those places are breeding grounds for Communists. They are training those kids to take us from the inside," he replied.

In Robert's mind the country was under siege, the world was under siege, and the good old US of A had to step in and save everyone. And anyone who wasn't willing to participate was a piece of shit.

This was very much on Robbie's mind as his nineteenth birthday galloped toward him. Would he be called to serve? If he was, would he go? He knew his mother had always dreamed of him going to college, of making something of himself. But his father did not feel too kindly about institutions of higher learning. They were hotbeds of unrest, of laziness, of sex, drugs, and rock 'n' roll, and there was no way in hell his hard-earned money was going to all of that. He'd done just fine graduating from the school of life, he always said. There was no better education than that. Robbie thought he might want to be a part of something that was bigger than himself; college seemed a way to do that without having to kill. Or be killed.

Mary was silent on the matter while her husband was in earshot; she would never let on, but she knew that Robert had wanted to go to college on the GI Bill. Instead, he had to get a job to support his new family. She'd been setting aside money each week since Robbie was born, something she learned from her own mother, who had handed Mary a roll of cash on her wedding day.

"Just in case," she said, looking at her daughter pointedly.

Although she wasn't sure what her mother meant, she held on to that money, tucking it in her underwear drawer where she knew Robert would never look. Each week she added a bit of her house money to the stack. She never thought much about what she would do with it until Robbie began talking about college. All at once Mary understood what her mother had meant: the money was so she could get out. But, like her mother, she chose to use it to get her child out. The thought filled her with a mixture of joy and sadness because she knew that in order for Robbie to go to college, he would have to leave and never come back. Maybe in time Robert would forgive him, but that would be a long time coming if it ever came at all.

Still, it was the right thing to do. Not only so Robbie could become something, but so that her son would be safely at home instead of halfway around the world, sleeping on the ground and killing people he had never met. There was enough in her stash to get him started. The rest she'd have to figure out as she went along.

Robbie was astonished when his mother presented him with the money one afternoon in early spring. He knew it was not the little bit of side money she gave him every year to do what he liked with, things that Robert would have considered wasteful. Her husband was not in favor of giving his son money to squander as he pleased. A gift on his birthday, something he wanted but did not need, was enough. But Mary wanted her son to experience the frivolous once in a while. She believed life was short and too often we defer joy for practicality.

When Robbie opened the envelope later, alone in his room, he gasped as the sheer volume of the bills. The note tucked inside explained the windfall. He smiled—a wistful smile because he knew how much she had sacrificed for him—and added it to his own stack, grown from saving every dollar his mother ever gave him.

He hugged her tightly the first moment they were alone. "I will do my best for you," he said.

"You always do," she replied.

Robbie began looking for colleges. His original criteria for choosing schools was "anywhere but here." Now he didn't want to be too far away so his mother could visit from time to time. He didn't think he'd be welcome home again.

Meanwhile the conflict in Vietnam dragged on with no end in sight. In May, four Kent State students protesting the war were killed by National Guardsmen. Robbie wondered if college was really safer. Some of his friends were ready to serve, enlisting as soon as the military would take them. May stretched into June, and July loomed like a dark shadow over the neighborhood. The draft lottery was coming; Robbie's future would be determined by the random selection of dates and numbers.

That night the family gathered around the television. Dinner had been cold cheese sandwiches and potato chips, which went largely untouched. Robbie sat in the corner of the couch chewing his left thumb until Mary took his hand. She reached for her husband's when they started plucking the red and blue plastic capsules from the bin. Her grip tightened as each birth date was called. Robert sat on the edge of his chair, leaning forward and keeping his eyes locked on the screen. Robbie held his breath as each pair was called, exhaling loudly afterward. It seemed like hours until April 21 was called.

It drew number eight.

There was silence as Mary shut the television off. They sat, contemplating the food on their plates, poking at it as daylight faded away and the room filled with darkness.

"It's an honor to serve, son," Robert said. There was a lack of conviction in his voice that did not go unnoticed.

Robbie nodded slowly but said nothing.

"What about college?" said Mary.

Robert got up and left the room.

"I don't know," said Robbie. But he did. His applications hadn't gone out yet. Deferments were about to end. College wasn't an option anymore. It was too late.

"What about..." Mary didn't finish, but Robbie understood. His money, the money for college, could take him as far as he needed to go.

"Maybe," he said, wondering what kind of person that would make him. Wondering if he could live with that person.

"But you can't go, Robbie," his mother pleaded. Her face was pale, and she looked terrified. She was terrified. "Things aren't going well over there. I don't want you to go."

"I'm not sure I have a choice. Why should I get to skip out when other people have to go?" He was scared and pale too.

A lump had formed in the pit of his stomach. He couldn't eat. He slept a lot for the next few days. He needed to know it was going to be okay, that he would be okay. There was no one to reassure him. He wanted to know what it would be like to be a soldier.

"Is it horrible to kill someone?" he asked his father.

Robert didn't look his son in the eye. "Just do what they tell you."

The orders came a couple of weeks later. It would be September.

It was a cold summer in their house. Mary jumped every time the phone rang or the doorbell buzzed. Robbie snapped at his mother when she asked him what he'd like for dinner.

Robert was nearly silent since the lottery. His wife and son moved like robots through their days. He watched. He knew this dance. He watched Mary, and his heart ached for her. He could see the worry in her eyes and the way it tugged at them, making her look older than she had weeks before. Her fear reminded him of his own mother, who was never the same after he went away. Or maybe she was the same but he wasn't. Maybe that was worse. She sent her son to war and got back a stranger. The bright, ambitious young man who left her home one sunny morning never returned. There was no visit from two men in uniform who regretted to inform her, but she had lost him just the same. Before the lottery, he'd felt a stab of pride at the idea of sending his son to serve his country. Now it wasn't an idea anymore. He knew what was waiting for his son and found he wanted none of it. He didn't want Mary to lose her only child, not to death and not to the person he would surely become if he survived. He didn't want it for himself either.

He was grateful that his son favored Mary, that he had her warmth and her caring. While Mary was pregnant, Robert had worried that the shadow of death he carried around with him would infect the baby. He feared he wouldn't be able to love his child.

Mary urged Robbie to quietly pack his things and disappear, to head north to safety. He would nod when she suggested it, but he dragged his feet. How dare he? How dare he not do anything to save his own life?

"This is your fault," she told her husband, stabbing her finger in his direction.

"What is my fault?" Robert stood up straighter and squared his shoulders.

"It's your fault that Robbie is going to Vietnam." She moved toward him and poked the finger into his chest. "He won't run because he thinks you won't respect him." She stepped in close and put her hands on his shoulders. "He thinks you won't forgive him," she said as she shoved him.

Robert stumbled backward. "He said that?" His voice squeaked like a teenager's.

"He didn't have to. I know my son." Mary spun on her heel and walked away.

The day grew closer. Mary barely spoke to either of them; her anger was a presence in the house, a fourth occupant, one they had to tiptoe around and try to pretend didn't exist. Robert grieved the change in his wife. He'd often thought about what would have become of him without her. She pulled him back from the edge. He knew he didn't make it all the way back, but he landed in a habitable place. He had been content with his life.

Worse than Mary's anger was Robbie's seeming indifference to his situation. Robert thought that he'd shut down, cut himself off from facing his future. He remembered that feeling. He took on the dread his son was trying not to feel.

But Robbie wasn't in denial. He simply hadn't decided what he would do yet. He could feel his mother's anger and even his father's worry, which surprised him. He'd imagined that Robert would actually be proud that his progeny was going off to serve his country. Almost happy about it. He was loathe to admit it, but his father's anxiety scared him to death. What was waiting for him over there? Was it as bad as it looked?

At night after everyone else was asleep, he would pull the weighty envelope of money from under his mattress and finger the stack, imagining himself running away and making a new life someplace pretty, like Vancouver. Then he'd feel a tug in his chest; he could never come home again.

In August, war protestors bombed Sterling Hall at the campus in Madison, killing one person.

"They march against death in a foreign country one day, then kill innocent people at home the next," Robert said. "Ungrateful little bastards. Love it or leave it!"

In this Robbie agreed with his father. He couldn't understand why peaceful protests had given way to the very violence and waste of life they were fighting against.

His report date was looming and he felt no closer to a decision. He hoped his father would tell him more, to prepare him for what was coming. Any other time Robert's silence would have been a gift, but no one else knew what he knew, what Robbie would soon know. At times he would catch himself staring at his dad, willing him to open up and reveal those secrets, but when Robert would look up from his newspaper or cup of coffee, Robbie would quickly avert his eyes.

Robert felt the longing coming from his boy, rolling toward him in anxious waves, tugging at his attention, but he could not make himself respond. He knew what his son wanted and he was unable to offer it. Putting words to the images that hovered in the back of his consciousness would make it all real again, and it would infect his home. And his child.

"Have you heard from Jim lately?" Robbie asked a friend one day. They were on the UW campus, on the lawn among long-haired college students sitting in for peace.

The friend shrugged. "Not since he was at Fort Campbell. I guess he got shipped out."

Robbie's stomach clenched. He felt nauseated.

The speaker, a young man with limp blond hair and an unkempt beard, raised his fist and his voice. "Peace now! Peace now!" People around them stood up and began pumping their fists and yelling along. "Peace now! Peace now!" A few minutes later there was a change, subtle at first, but then unmistakable. The cries became louder and more angry. "Peace now! Peace now!" The crowd began to stand.

"What the hell is going on?" he said. His friend shrugged again.

The day came. Robbie woke early and finished packing his things, trying to ignore the churning in his stomach and the way his hands shook as he tucked a picture of his mother into the pocket of his duffle bag. He had no idea what his life was going to become, but he knew he was starting over from today.

"I love you," was all Mary could say. Her hands shook as she straightened his collar and smoothed his shirt. She hugged him tightly. When she let go, there was a wet spot on his shoulder. He would take more than just her heart with him.

The drive to the bus station was silent except for Mary's occasional sniffles. Robbie looked out the window, noticing the way the light hit the trees, the color of the sky. He didn't think home had ever looked so beautiful. He wanted to remember every leaf, every blade of grass.

They stood at the station, surrounded by other families handing their boys over to their country. Tension and anxiety mixed with the smell of hay and wildflowers that wafted on the breeze. It was quiet, nearly silent, as each person listened to the narration in their own minds:

It's going to be okay. I'm scared. Why me? Am I going to die? I'm losing my baby.

The quiet was shattered by the voice of a man in an Army uniform. He held a clipboard and began to shout names. One by one the young men said hasty goodbyes to their families and scurried on the bus as the man screamed at them. Robbie's name was called.

"Take care of yourself, son," Robert said, trying to keep his voice steady. He shook Robbie's hand, then pulled him in for a one-armed embrace. Mary stood behind them, hand clamped over her mouth.

They watched him walk away.

The families stood around long after the bus had left. No one could bear to leave. After a while Robert took Mary's hand and led her to the car. He tried to speak to her, to comfort her, as they headed back to their empty house, but she wouldn't even look at him. She stared out the window, seeing nothing. Robert stopped trying and turned on the radio. Mary leaned forward and snapped it off.

Their neighborhood looked the same as it had earlier, neat lawns and small, well-tended homes. The trees that lined the street, the ones that Mary had fallen in love with so many years ago, covered the road in deep shadow. Her shoulders tensed as they approached home. The house, she thought. It's not home anymore. She shivered, and Robert tried to take her hand again. She lifted her left hand and began to chew on her thumb, still looking straight ahead. He opened the front door and his wife flew by him, her usually light steps replaced by the angry staccato of her heels on the wood floor as she made her way to the kitchen. It was lunchtime.

As Mary fixed their midday meal, her shoulders softened and her breathing deepened. The ache in her throat receded although her mouth was still set in a hard line. Bread, mustard, ham, swiss. Bread, mustard, ham, swiss. My baby. Cut, cut, cut. Pickle, pickle, pickle, chips. She set the kitchen table as she had every afternoon for almost twenty years, wiped her hands on the flour sack apron at her waist, then walked into the living room to fetch her husband. His chair was empty, the television dark. Down the hall she could see the empty bathroom. She made her way to the bedroom she and Robert still shared and saw him, standing by his side of the bed, holding something in his hand. She saw traces of tears on his cheeks as he stared at the papers he held. He pushed them toward her, then hid his face behind his hands as his chest heaved silently.

Mary looked at what was in her hand: an envelope full of cash, a *Manual for Draft-Age Immigrants to Canada*, and a note to Robbie from her husband.

"Please go," it said.

Going Home

My parents still have sex. I know this because the guest room in their condo is right next to their bedroom. I have been here for a week and it's happened at least three times. They're 75. My mother makes a lot of noise, which is horrifying, but thankfully my father does not because that would be more horrifying. I'm here because it's what you do when you have aging parents and are constantly reminded that they could go at any moment. I just hope it doesn't happen while they're fucking.

Six months ago they sold my childhood home and moved into this "active adult" community. Initially I laughed at the "active adult" part because I always thought of these places as the last train station before death but as it turns out my parents are getting more action than I am, so... yeah.

Going home after you've been away for years is like watching a movie you've seen a hundred times;

everything is so familiar but you don't belong to any of it.

The condo is in Boynton Beach, Florida, only a few miles from my childhood home. I don't admit this to anyone, but I dread going back. As much as I want to be near my family, I stay away, and I'm at a loss to explain why. There is something about this place that tugs at my soul. The smell of blacktop softening in the sun or the whisper of wind through a stand of Australian Pines brings back moments long forgotten and those I'd rather forget. My parents are perfectly content coming to visit me, so I often ask myself why I keep coming back. Why go someplace that just makes me sad?

Maybe it's important to revisit places from the past so you can make peace with those memories, to put old ghosts to rest.

"Can I make you some eggs, sweetie?" Mom says to me on the first morning of my visit, the morning after the first night of my visit. Her hair is messy in a way that is undeniably sexy, and she's wearing a shortie nightgown with a kimono-style silk robe over it. She's still got great legs. I can't look at her legs because I only imagine them wrapped around my father's waist and... no.

"Sure," I say, stumbling toward the coffee pot, pretending to be very interested in what I am doing and wondering if my parents have any Bailey's in the house. I don't think I can get through this trip stone cold sober.

My father strides into the kitchen looking like he invented water and plants a big kiss on my mother's lips. I swear I throw up a little in my mouth. Were they like this when I was a kid? The thought of their seventy-something bodies doing things to each other makes me shudder.

In theory it's great though, right? Knowing you can have fulfilling sex at any age should be encouraging, and it probably would be if it were someone else's parents. If I heard your parents screwing in the wee hours the next morning I'd be throwing a fist bump at your dad and nudging your mom knowingly and you'd be the one swallowing bile.

WHEN WE ARE away from the people we love they exist in suspended animation. We expect them to be right where we left them, standing in the doorway, waving. It always comes as a shock that they actually have lives, that they grow and progress in our absence. When we return to them, full of our own triumphs and failures, we marvel that they've been able to manage to craft a whole existence without us.

My parents blossomed once their nest was emptied. Mom went back to school and got her Ph.D in American Studies and teaches a Pop Culture course that has a waiting list every semester at the local university. This is a woman who, in the '80s, questioned wearing leg warmers outside of a ballet studio and was horrified when I cut the neck out of my brand-new sweatshirt. My father retired from his job at IBM. I really have no idea what he did there, but it had nothing to do with typewriters. He took up photography, shows his shots of Florida wildlife at local art fairs, and earns enough to finance several vacations a year.

We go home again expecting things to be the same, to look the same, to smell the same, to taste the same. We want—we need—a touchstone to the past to reassure us that everything does not have an expiration date.

I'm always amazed that that things keep changing even when other things feel the same. I'm haunted by some of what remains, yet am disappointed when anything is not as I remembered. Mom still buys Special K cereal, which I used to love. Three days into my trip, I pour myself a bowl.

"What happened to the cereal?" I ask, looking for the tiny flakes from my youth.

"They made the flakes bigger," she says nonchalantly.

"Why?"

She shrugs. "Don't know."

I pour the cereal back in the box and sigh.

Mom has gotten rid of the plates we used when I was growing up, replacing them with heavy stoneware in a pattern that reminds me of Spanish tiles rendered in blue. They are gorgeous, and I hate them. I want the scratched melamine dishes with the faded, wheat-colored flowers, and I want to eat meatloaf with ketchup alongside mashed potatoes and those flaccid green beans from a can off of them. I embrace change, but only in my own life. I want my parents' existence to remain the same, but it hasn't. They haven't. The first thing I noticed was that they look like someone's grandparents. Mom looks amazing and Dad is still handsome, but they don't look like my parents anymore.

But not everything has changed. My mother is still best friends with my Aunt Joey, who is still a piece of work. Joey is everything you shouldn't be but so want to be. Or is that just me? She smokes, she drinks too much, she says whatever pops into her mind, and she can hold a grudge until it turns to dust. But she will do anything for those she loves without reservation. She's got a giant heart to match her big mouth.

We have the obligatory girls' night, complete with too many cocktails. Mom and Joey get drunk, but I do not. We're at Joey's, in the same house where she has lived as far back as I can remember, a place filled with memories both bitter and sweet. It's late, and we're cleaning up the kitchen. I come into the room laden with plates to find my mother standing at the sink, washing dishes, while Joey is on the floor, between Mom's legs, passed out and snoring.

"Don't you think we should get her off of the floor?" I ask.

Mom waves me off. "She's too heavy. I'd rather get this done and just move her once when we put her to bed."

Makes sense to me—maybe I am a little drunk—so I keep clearing the dining room table. When everything is dry and put away, we take Joey to bed.

"You take her feet, and I'll take her shoulders," I say as I bend down to lift Joey up. I suddenly understand what they mean by dead weight. Plus my mother weighs all of 90 pounds and isn't as strong as she used to be, so lifting Joe off of the floor isn't going to happen.

"Let's just each grab a foot and drag her into the bedroom," Mom says. Something in her tone tells me this is not the first time she's done this. I grab a bare left foot.

Mom shrugs.

The tile floors make surprisingly easy work of hauling an 120-pound woman across the house. We position her next to the bed and manage to rouse her enough to get her tucked in for the night.

On the way back to my parents' place I ask my mother if she thinks that maybe she and Joey drink too much.

"Absolutely," she answers. "But we'll be dead soon, so who cares as long as nobody's driving?"

I nod because what else can I do?

"Thank God for Uber, or I'd never leave the house after dark," she adds.

"Can't you drive at night?" I ask. Until this trip I hadn't realized what a big deal that was. When the condo women are gossiping about widowers, the ability to drive at night seems more important than wearing pants that are not pulled up to their armpits.

"I can drive just fine, but after cocktail hour, it's safer not to."

"Why do you drink so much?"

"It's not that I drink a lot, only a glass or two of wine usually. It just hits me funny these days."

"But you drink every day?"

"Sure. Why not?"

I really don't have a response for that. She's nearly 80 years old, who am I to tell her what to do?

"I'll be dead soon, so I might as well enjoy myself."

"Why do you keep saying that?"

"What? That I'll be dead soon? Because I will. I just feel it. It's no big deal. It happens to everyone."

My father is far less nonchalant about my mother's impending demise. He has not prepared to outlive her.

"I don't even know where the checkbook is," he tells me.

"Do you still use checks?"

"I have no idea. See? She can't go first. I keep telling her that."

Is this what happens in marriage? If you stay together long enough, you eventually start talking about dying? No wonder so many people get divorced.

MY MARRIAGE WAS a mistake from day one. I was on some weird timetable where I thought I needed to be married by 25, and when it started getting close and Michael was the only one in the vicinity, I decided he was The One. He was not. We were perfect for a brief fling but crap for anything long term. Compatible in bed but not in life. I was sorry to see him go while at the same time being relieved.

I have yet to actually find The One, though I have thoroughly enjoyed the search.

My younger sister is happily married with three kids, and my older brother is happily married and happily childless. I have no children either, and I am not sorry about that. The biggest impression that my childhood left on me was that children steal from their parents, particularly their mothers, at least it looked that way to me. Mom spent a lot of time tending to the needs of three children and her husband with very little on her own pursuits. As the middle child—not doted on by my parents but not expected to help them either—I'm used to answering mostly to myself and maybe that's why I feel the way I do. Funny how that works, how the uniqueness of each of us colors our experiences. Same parents, same role models, and different outcomes.

"Not everyone is cut out for marriage," my mother always reminds me. "There's nothing wrong with it. You really don't have the temperament for compromise. You've always been too independent, and now you've been alone too long. You cannot share your life with someone else."

She reminds me that I have never needed anyone else, and men cannot handle that. I see now that my mother is the same way. She went back to school because she wanted something that was just for her. My father didn't understand it, and I remember that was one of the low points of their relationship. Dad was resentful that Mom's life seemingly wasn't enough for her, that he wasn't enough for her. And he was right; one person can't be everything to another. I think he was afraid she'd leave him, but the relationship survived, and it was because my mother wanted it. She willed it to be so. She had to hold that part of herself back until her kids didn't need her anymore, then fight to get my father to accept the very woman he married all those years ago.

I'd rather be by myself. Alone doesn't mean lonely; I'd much rather be alone than be lonely with someone sleeping beside me. I wonder out loud why people stay in marriages that feel that way.

"Marriage isn't a straight line, my love," my mother says. "Sometimes you're in sync with each other and sometimes you're not. It changes. And it takes work, especially when you don't feel like it."

"Have you ever felt that way with Dad?"

"Absolutely. Particularly when you kids were little and I had primary responsibility for taking care of you. Nothing makes you feel more isolated than spending the day with no one to have a real conversation with and then having the only one you can talk to come home too tired to bother. I nearly left him a few times."

"Really?"

"Yes. But don't tell him that. He doesn't know. I just toyed with the idea."

"Why didn't you leave?"

"Where was I going to go that would be any different? If I met someone else it would be glorious in the beginning, like it always is. It was that way with your father. But it would change, and I'd be in the same situation with someone else. You can't run away from it. You just have to choose to power through it and wait for the next stage to begin. It always comes around if there is love and respect. You don't always have to be wild about each other. Sometimes just liking each other's company is enough."

This is simultaneously comforting and sad. The whole trip has been. That love endures, and that maybe when you reach the end of your life you are ready for it to be done gives me hope. That your expectations diminish along with your eyesight? Not so much.

Maybe it's just me. I am prone to wistfulness. Always have been. When I look back on my childhood, I can see it was tinged with the patina of melancholy, an ache in my chest that I still don't quite understand, a longing I cannot name. Coming back home always reminds me of how happy I am that I've left. I'm far more content where I landed than where I launched. I'm sure a therapist could unearth something to provide an explanation, but I am not inclined to do that work. Denial is a tranquil place, and I see no reason to leave it.

I WATCH MY parents for the rest of the week, the ebb and flow of their connection. Sometimes they are a unit, riding on the same wavelength like when my Uncle John, my mother's brother, goes on a political rant. They look at each other and you can see them mentally rolling their eyes. Not this again. Other times they seem to live in different realities, like when Dad suggested going to the new Mexican restaurant down the street, knowing his wife of over

50 years despises Mexican food. The look on her face—Do you even know me?—made me laugh, but it was sad too.

Do we get so caught up in our own thing that we don't see each other any more? Or do we just want what we want and hope the other will acquiesce if we keep trying?

Maybe coming home is difficult because it forces me to come face to face with my shit. Any time I visit, I learn something new about myself.

Family is the running water that shapes us into who we are; as we move into the world we find other rivers to hone our rough edges, but the essence of us is where we come from.

From the distance I've placed between those I love and myself, I can see the cracks in the facade, the things that I don't like as well as those that I do, and I can't tell if I'm the things I don't like or the ones that I do or both at the same time.

Maybe you go home out of obligation, maybe you go for answers, maybe out of nostalgia. Or maybe you go home just because it's home.

A Pause In Our Estrangement

Here's what I want to do for you," your email says. "I want to give you one week away from life, away from everything, just me and you."

I am dying, the reason for the offer. We haven't been together in a very long time; our lives diverged one fall night 30 years ago and barreled forward until we came here. Now my time is short and yours is no longer bound to the wife I'd always hoped you couldn't have loved more than you loved me. You lost her unexpectedly, and it left you reeling, and now you're spinning anew with the news of my imminent departure.

Is this pause in our estrangement your gift to me or to yourself, a balm to the wound her death left? I don't care, really. I don't care because all these years the memory of you was a place I could escape to when things got hard, so why not now? Why not one last time, why not make new memories that will sustain me until the breath leaves my body?

So I agree and am immediately nervous about the person you will see when you arrive. Will you recognize me? Has time been as kind to me as it's been to you? This disease is beginning to take its toll but I am still me and I hope you will see that.

This offer is about more than a week at the beach, I know. This is how we close the circle, you and me. You were my first love, Mark, the first to touch the most intimate places in my soul—now you will be the last. This is the real goodbye.

The day comes and I wake up and shower and dress and then all of sudden I'm standing in front of you and you are glorious. The gods have looked down on you, have blessed you—you are more gorgeous at 50 than you were at 20. My breath eludes me. I am suddenly self-conscious of the scars you haven't yet seen, the marks of motherhood and modern medicine and time itself. It doesn't occur to me that you'd have scars of your own. I can't speak, I can only rush forward and put my arms around you and bury my face in your chest. You smell the same, and the baggage of 30 years is lifted from my shoulders and I am young again and in love as long as I can stay right here. We part, and I touch your face and run my hands down your shoulders and arms and capture your hands in mine.

"Hi," I say.

"Hi," you reply.

I very much want to kiss you but don't.

"We've a long drive," you say.

I nod and let go of your hands. We pack up the trunk together, and then I slide into your car, a pristine cocoon of quiet confidence scented with vanilla and leather. This vehicle is present-day you, the culmination of all of those aspirations you had in college, those dreams you'd whisper in my ear about, the plans you said you'd include me in.

The silence as we start out is awkward, and I hate that. I remember so many weekend mornings where our only communication was a passing touch or a look. The quiet between us was warm and safe, not needing to be filled, but now, with the hum of the engine the only sound, everything that we haven't said hangs in the space between us, the weight of it almost unbearable. You look at me out of the corner of your eye and reach out to take my hand. I feel a tingle where your skin touches mine, and the tension between us eases.

"Are you okay? I mean really?" you ask. You still know me, know that I will tell anyone else that I am always okay even if I'm not.

"No," I say, looking out the window at the gas stations, cheap motels, and fast-food places that are flying by at 70 mph.

You nod, squeeze my hand, and say no more, leaving space for me to fill or not, to let you in or keep you at a distance. I do not like to be vulnerable—you know this—but you are also the only one I was really able to be vulnerable with. And look how that turned out. Still, I know I will tear open all my wounds for you like I always did. In the quiet and dark of night, drunk on oxytocin and maybe some wine, I will open to you like a flower. This is how you learned all my secrets. And I yours.

Ten more miles down the road, I turn to you.

"Are *you* okay?"

You smile, but it doesn't light up your eyes like it usually does.

"No," you say.

I nod and squeeze your hand, then lean over to turn on the radio. You grab your phone and in a few taps Tracy Chapman's "Fast Car" fills the empty space between us.

"Remember when I used to make you mix tapes? I made this playlist for you."

I lean back in my seat and close my eyes, letting the music take me back to a time when life was full and still ahead of me. Of us.

To SAY I loved you would have been an understatement. I adored you, worshipped you, the sun rose and set on you. For that brief time you were my world, and there was nothing more I wanted or needed. You saw me, and you genuinely liked and admired what you saw. You loved me, not just the image of me that you had in your head, a reflection of what you wanted other people to think of you. That was new to me. I had little experience with men, and what I had only served to inform me that I was only good for one thing. But you changed that. You fell in love with me, and it was everything I could have wished for.

We were so young, so hopeful. Love was a new adventure, and it was just the two of us with nothing to get in the way, no baggage from past relationships, no kids, no stress. And maybe that's why first love clings to the edges of our souls—it is the foundation on which all other love is built, the blueprint our hearts yearn to follow. It is, at least at its beginning, a singular perfect thing. Love in its youth is the stuff of nostalgia and longing, intense and more real than anything you'd ever imagined. And when it ends, the fall is devastating.

THE PLAYLIST LASTS an hour and a half, the entirety of our trip, a fact not lost on me. You were always able to anticipate things that never occurred to me. I wouldn't have expected our first hours to be awkward, to be at a loss for words. Even though you don't look the same, when I look at you I see the boy I fell in love with. I see you as I knew you. My heart sees yours in your eyes and recognizes it. But it feels different. We are not the same people at all. The part of me that aches for you is the remnant of that girl that loved the boy you were. I love the memory of you, the feeling of loving you. You, the person who stands before me today, are a stranger. The music both fills the silence and bridges past and present.

Our home for the week is as grand as your car. You're showing off for me. And I like that you want to show off for me even though you could have pitched a tent on the beach for us and I would be just as content. Your company has always been enough; you were always enough, no matter what your father would have had you believe.

You lead me inside and show me to my room, separate from yours. Now you have surprised me. I thought—expected—that you'd brought me here for one last fling, but you're leaving that question open. I can't read the expression on your face as you guide me through the door. I can feel the heat rising in my cheeks; I'm embarrassed by my assumption and am certain that you know exactly what I was thinking and enjoy my discomfort. The twinkle in your eye gives you away. I let it pass unacknowledged.

"This is the owner's suite," you say, placing my suitcase on the luggage rack at the end of the king-size bed. You pick up a remote on the nightstand and push a button. The sunscreen at the window whirrs to life and rolls back to reveal an expansive view of the beach and ocean, a private pool and spa. I look at you and think that maybe your goal isn't to impress me but to spoil me. A fullness grows in my chest, warm and familiar, painful and bittersweet, a long-dormant seed coming to bloom again.

"It's beautiful. Thank you," I say, biting back the "you didn't have to do this for me" which would have accompanied it when we were together. Back then I didn't know I deserved nice things, perhaps one of the reasons we didn't make it. I'd always believed you were too good for me, too good to last, so I made it true.

Tears, lying in wait for hours, spring forth the moment you leave. I am overcome but can't decide if it's with happiness, regret, or sorrow. Probably all of that and more, I think as I lie down on the bed, staring out the window until I fall asleep.

The sun is low in the sky when my eyes open again. Your weight on the side of the bed, the warmth of your fingers on my shoulder awaken me. I'm disoriented and surprised by your presence and look at you with a mixture of wonder and disbelief.

"Dinner's ready," you say in a quiet voice, the voice that I hear in my memories telling me that I am beautiful and loved, and then telling me that you're leaving without me. Your voice. You are here but my brain can't quite add up how and why. Am I dreaming? Or was I dreaming before, when you were gone?

There are several seconds of each day, the moments after my eyes first open in the morning, that I do not know that I have cancer. In those moments I am simply my senses—smell, touch, hear—no feelings. And then the weight settles back into my chest and I struggle to name this dread and then remember that I am dying. Now, with you sitting beside me on the bed, I do not know that we've not spent a lifetime together. I sit up, ready to curl into your arms, to kiss your perfect mouth, and then my stomach clenches, and I remember that you are no longer mine and that I am dying.

I nod, knowing that speaking is not possible in the moment. The revelation must settle, work its way down into my legs and feet, my arms and hands, make itself at home in my body once again before

I can be myself and not a mass of emotional nerve endings collapsing in on itself because the pain is unbearable.

"On the terrace," you say, standing up.

You leave the room and I stare out the window at the waves crashing on the beach until I can heave myself off the bed.

By the time I join you outside, I've found my smile in a memory and it crosses my face, as easy as an exhale.

I couldn't ask for a more perfect evening, nor dream of it. My favorite foods, my favorite music, my favorite person. If I don't allow myself to think too much, I can be in our past, young and hopelessly in love, more life in front of me than behind me. I can forget the things I don't want to remember.

When I've had too much wine and the sun has finished its descent into the waves, I curl up in my chair and regard you, tilting my head to the left, a silent signal designed to will you into my personal space. You smile at me but don't move. I straighten my head and narrow my eyes. What do you want? Why am I here?

You can still read my mind. "I'm not sure what this is going to be." You speak softly and I am reminded of the first time we made love and the gentle reassurances you whispered into my ear. There is love and genuine concern there, but I'm unsure for whom—for me, for you, or for your dead wife? Perhaps all of us. And this annoys me—can't this be all about me? Because it feels like my life has never been about me, not until the cancer, although it's not really about me but the disease as it turns out. I want this to be about me because it's the last time anything ever will be.

"Does it need a label?" I ask, trying to soften my tone, tamp down the need that is threatening to burst out from my mouth and my eyes and my soul. "You brought me here. This was your idea. What did you want it to be?"

You shake your head. "Dunno. I guess I thought things would fall naturally into place, but…" You cover your eyes with your right hand. Hiding tears. You never liked to look vulnerable either, even with me. You shrugged off the arrows thrown at you by your parents, recounting them with almost clinical detachment, but sometimes I'd wake in the middle of the night and feel your shoulders shake as you cried under cover of darkness, your quiet sobs masked by the drone of the box fan in the corner of the bedroom. I'd curl into your back, pretending to still be asleep and trying not to cry with you.

"You miss her," I say.

"Yes." You sniffle and wipe your face with a napkin. "And you too." You look at me, waiting for a response.

"Do you?"

"Yes," you say, nodding slowly. "I've missed you every day since we split up. I missed you when I met Anne, I missed you when I fell in love with her, and I missed you when I married her. I loved... I love her with all of my heart, except for the part that belongs to you."

I look down and see my hands tightly clasped in my lap. I am not prepared to hear this. I've never considered that you ever continued to love me. I had never considered that this week would be anything but nostalgia, a respite from the grief and pain that has taken hold of our lives. The thought that you still love me should make me giddy, and it does, but it also devastates me with the sadness of all that wasted time, so I find myself not feeling much at all. I am numb, my heart paralyzed by the conflict.

"Grace." A simple declaration. A plea. My name. Which is it?

I put my hand up to stop you. "I can't right now, okay? What you just told me is huge, you know that, right? I have to sit with it for a while. Tomorrow, okay?" I am suddenly exhausted. It takes every ounce of energy I have left to haul myself out of the chair and take a step toward you. I touch your face with the side of my index finger, and a familiar jolt runs through me. "Thank you for dinner," I say.

You help me back to my room, where I fall into a dreamless sleep.

There is a rapping at the door. I open one eye and reach over to tap my phone to life. It's 2:30 a.m.

"Come in?" I am unsure where I am or who is on the other side of the door.

The shades are drawn, only thin slivers of moonlight escaping at the edges, throwing everything into dark shadows, shapes, suggestions of things rather than the things themselves. A head pokes into the room. "Grace?" Your voice catapults me into the present and my throat constricts. Why are you here?

"Yes?"

"I can't sleep."

I regard the outline of your head, the still-thick hair sticking out like a halo. I pull back the covers and pat the bed beside me. You quickly slide in and get comfortable so that I don't wake up all the way. I fall back to sleep feeling the warmth radiating from you and the faintest hint of your scent.

The dream feels utterly real—I can feel, see, hear, taste—and in it I am light and free and healthy. We are us, but a new us shaped by a long absence and other loves come and gone. We know that our souls are bound together, connected over many lifetimes, and that we will always end up together. A joy I haven't felt in so long fills me, drawing light into my body and tears from eyes.

I am awakened, disoriented and wet-faced, by sunlight finding its way into the room and the sound of you stirring in your sleep. In the back of my mind I know that these next few moments are precious and should be savored, but I don't yet know why. My dream still stirring inside me, I slide over and push my breasts into your back and my arm around your waist. You grab my hand and pull it up tight to your chest, and we sleep for a bit longer.

The light is stronger when my eyes open next. You are softly kissing the palm of my hand, no doubt aware of the delicate invitation you are sending yet unaware that I'm awake to receive it. My body begins to respond until my mind awakens and I remember.

"Don't." My voice sounds meek and unsure.

"I'm sorry."

"No," I say. "Don't be. I just..." My throat is choked with tears and for the first time in a long time, I let myself cry.

You turn over and pull me into your arms. I wrap my body around yours, bury my face in your neck and cry while you kiss the top of my head and run your hand up and down my back. You are the cure and the sickness, the cause and the remedy.

"We need to talk," I say, tears spent and drying on my face.

You nod and squeeze me tighter.

THE LAST TIME I cried in your arms was the last time I saw you. Graduation was looming, and I was terrified; I had no idea what to do next. Overwhelmed with thoughts of the future, I showed up at your place with a bottle of wine and my heart on my sleeve. I wanted you to tell me it would be okay, to tell me that we would face whatever the future held together. What you told me was that you had been accepted to grad school on the other side of the country and that you'd be going alone.

"I need to put my life in order," you said. "I have to do this part alone."

You held me for so long I almost thought you'd changed your mind. But then you took my hand and led me to your car and drove me home. My last memory of you is turning back and seeing you standing in the parking lot, watching me walk away.

I TAKE MY coffee on the patio, away from you so that I can think. Why I feel conflicted is a mystery to me. What possible difference could it make now? I want you—I never stopped—so why not? Who gets hurt here? Me, I tell myself. Could I hurt any more than I already do, I counter. It seems so silly to be worried about heartbreak at this point. My heart has been torn in half and here I am, given the chance to live in a moment I thought would never come and I hesitate. You would think cancer would have taught me better.

Maybe it's not heartbreak but humiliation that concerns me. Why are we here? Do you feel guilty? Is this about pity? Or would you have come to me after your wife's death if I were healthy? I think this is what plagues me. I don't want you that way. I want you the way I remember you, the way I remember us and I know that it is not possible and so I hesitate.

Can I be okay with what is rather than what I'd like it to be? And do I need to know what it is at all?

You leave me alone long enough that I don't want to be alone anymore, and then you appear as if by magic. Once you told me that you could feel what I was feeling, even if we weren't in the same room. I hadn't remembered that until now. When we were together I believed it was because you knew me better than I knew myself, that you knew what I wanted and needed even when I didn't, but now? I know there are too many things that defy rational explanation. Whether it's a spiritual connection between us or simply an instinct perfected over time no longer matters, you are here exactly when I need you to be.

"Gracie," you say in that achingly gentle voice. I'm curled up in the corner of a shaded couch, watching the waves go in and out, and you come and sit so close to me that my feet, tucked up under me as I lean on the armrest, are touching your thigh. I feel your warmth and the prickle of hair on my soles. There is something else too, a tension that wasn't here yesterday. I feel it so acutely that I cannot even look at you because I'm afraid I'll be overwhelmed. You reach out and put your hand, palm up, on my thigh. I hesitate.

"Please." That's all you ever had to say to me to make me bend to your will. This time I resist.

But only for a moment.

The way my hand fits into yours nearly breaks me, so familiar and yet so new. Even with my eyes closed I can see you, how you are sitting, the look on your beautiful face. I don't know what I am waiting for. Stop thinking, Grace, just feel. Feel every damn thing.

I set my mug down and shift so that I am leaning into you, my right hand still holding your left, my head on your shoulder. Minutes pass without words, but our bodies are speaking to each other. Then your hand lets go of mine and slides around my back to my hip, pulling me closer still. You kiss the top of my head, and your right arm moves around my waist so that I am wrapped up in you.

There's so much I want to ask you, so much I cannot understand even now after so much time, so much life has passed and taught me its lessons, cleared my vision, and informed my memories, but right now there's only one thing I need to know.

"Why did you ask me here?"

You don't answer, but I feel your whole body pull tight.

"It's okay," I say, kissing your shoulder. "You can tell me anything."

"It's not that," you say, shifting away slightly. "I'm not sure I should tell you."

"Is there such a thing at this point?" I pull my head away from your body and turn your chin toward me with my finger. "Do you think there's anything you could say that I haven't already imagined?

Is there anything you can tell me that would break my heart more than when you left me?"

"It's not you I'm afraid for. It's me." You bite your lip, the way you did right before you told me you loved me for the first time, and right before you told me goodbye for the last.

"Tell me."

"I still love you. I never stopped."

These are words I've wanted to hear for decades, words that would have set my world right at any given time but now just make me angry. "You never stopped? Seriously? You went on with your life and married someone else and had a whole life without me, but you never stopped loving me? I struggled for years to get my life together without you, to be happy without you, to just be without you, and I didn't have to? You could have come back to me and we could have had a life together instead of you marrying her? I wouldn't have had to carry your rejection around, trying to ignore my pain?" I'm sitting up now, tears streaming from my eyes, all the anger I'd directed at myself for not being enough now focused on you. "This cancer?" I say, pointing my finger at my chest, then back at you. "This is your fault.

Holding all of this in for so long, that's what gave me this thing." I stand up. "How dare you?" I leave you sitting there, pale and stricken, tears springing to your eyes.

FOUR YEARS AFTER graduation, I ran into one of our old friends in the grocery store, the one where I worked. I had yet to find my way, so I drifted from job to job, still living in my parents' house, spinning in circles without you.

She told me that she'd kept in touch with you, and that you'd found the perfect Silicone Valley job and met the perfect Silicon Valley woman whom you were about to marry. She told me that you were happy and that you told her to say hello if she should ever run into me. After she left, I went in the back to take my break, breathing into a paper bag and waiting for my heart to shatter.

I PACE THE floor in my room, occasionally falling to my knees and sobbing, then pulling myself together and pacing again. I am furious. I am haunted by what might have been. I am gutted.

You don't come after me, and I cannot decide whether or not you should or what I would do if you did.

My phone rings—my daughter, checking on me like she does every day. I force a smile so it creeps into my voice, placating her. Mom's okay, I can live my life for another 24 hours. She's a good girl, the best thing I ever did, equal parts me—whimsy and wonder—and her father—brilliant and brave. She's a testament, a reminder that no matter how it feels, my life was not wasted without you. The call ends with I love you's and I'm left sitting on the floor, head back, eyes closed, trying to center. Can I forgive you? Can I take this time for the gift that it is and just lean into it, extracting memories to sustain me until the cancer finally wins? Or do I let resentment creep in and fuel the rogue cells invading my body, hastening the inevitable? A laugh escapes me. Are those the only options, Grace? Black or white? Good or bad? Right or wrong?

My return to the patio surprises you; I see hope flash in your eyes. That's good because I'm here to make peace—with you, with our pasts. I stop for a moment and look at you. I always enjoyed looking at you. That's how we met, wasn't it? Me looking at you until you felt me looking at you, then you looking at me until I blushed and retreated to the ladies' room? One deep breath and then I cross to where you're sitting and settle in next to you, making sure we're touching wherever we can. My hand slides easily into yours as I look into your eyes.

"I don't have time to be mad at you," I say. "I don't have time to be sad about us. We have now, and it's just going to have to be enough."

"I..."

I put my finger to your lips. "I don't want to talk to you right now," I say, replacing my finger with my own lips.

Later I am lying in bed, looking out at the sand and the ocean but not really seeing them, my breathing deep and easy, my mind finally quiet except for the sound of the waves rushing in and out. You are asleep beside me, pulled tight against my back, legs tangled in mine, your arm slung around my waist. I do nothing but breathe and feel, memorizing this moment and the ones before it. This is what I want to carry with me for the rest of my days. We've been apart so long I can hardly remember what it was like making love with you then. I get flashes that are mostly feelings, the novelty of sleeping with my skin touching yours, the awakening of intimacy.

"Where are you?" you whisper. You kiss my shoulder and nuzzle my neck and suddenly I'm self-conscious of my hair, once long and abundant, now just the first few gray and silver inches of growth reclaiming what chemo took from me. You loved that I shed regularly, leaving hairs on everything you owned—you'd said you got to carry pieces of me with you all the time.

"There," I say absently.

"Yeah."

The waves rush in and back out. Our breathing is in sync with the water and each other. There are no other sounds for a long stretch.

"There are things I need to tell you," you say finally. "Things I want you to know... when you're ready."

"Uh huh."

We fall asleep.

Night has always been my favorite time, the darkness enveloping me, giving me cover. It's easy to hide in the dark, be alone even if there are other people nearby. As the week progresses, we are becoming increasingly nocturnal. I express concern for you, having to shift back into the daytime world when our time here is done. Me? I may just stay this way. It suits me, and I am making room for things that suit me these days, regardless of how they fit into anyone else's perceptions. I do what I want. And what I want—for now—is to swim in the dark, quiet hours of a new day. When I tire of movement, you coax me into the hot tub where I sit facing you in your lap, wrap my arms around you, put my head on your shoulder and am still but for the rise and fall of your chest as you breathe.

We've spoken very little of the past. I know you need to tell me that something you mentioned; I've not been ready to hear it, but I can feel it vibrating in your body, looking for release. I need to give you that, I know, but I fear if I do the tenuous hold I have on you will evaporate, and I've not been ready to open my hand to release you.

As we sit in silence and stillness, I feel the need welling in you again, and this time I cannot ignore it.

"Tell me," I say, quietly so as not to break the spell. I watch the candles you've dotted the patio with flicker in the ocean breeze, holding my breath.

You release me from your arms and place your hands on my shoulders, attempting to push me back so that we are looking at each other. "I need to look at you."

I shake my head. "No." What if I can't face this? What if I need time?

"Please."

I bury my face between your shoulder and neck, breathing you in for a moment before I comply.

"I never wanted to break up with you. I just needed some time to get myself together. You weren't the only one freaking out about the future. I wasn't used to depending on anyone else. I always figured things out by myself. And how could I help you if I couldn't get my own shit together?

"I didn't get to tell you all of this because you broke down and I felt horrible and then you wanted to leave. I tried calling you, I came around to your place. Do you remember? You wouldn't see me, you wouldn't talk to me. Your friend Tracey cornered me one day and told me that you didn't want anything more to do with me and that I should just leave you alone. So I did. I loved you so I left you alone hoping you'd find your way back to me. I asked Tracey to tell you I loved you and that I didn't want it to be over. Did she tell you that?"

I shake my head. She hadn't even told me she'd confronted you. All I'd known is that you stopped trying to see me, stopped trying to get in touch with me, and that the world as I knew it had ended.

"She didn't tell me anything," I said, swallowing a whole new batch of tears and struggling to find something else to say, but what could I say? "I'm so sorry."

You put your forehead on mine and close your eyes. "So I am I."

There's nothing more to say, I realize. There's nothing that will repair what's past, that will undo what's been done. Maybe we would have worked out, maybe we would have ended up hating each other and my last memories of you would be tainted with anger. The only thing we can do is be here now, and feel what we feel now, and make these new memories together and carry them with us until we—and they—are gone. Instead of talking I simply feel, hoping that it transfers to you where our bodies are touching, seeping out through my skin. We sit with our heads together for a long time, breathing in tandem, existing together in the moment.

I am concentrating on the sound of your breath, the heat coming from you, your smell mixed with chlorine from the water, and the roar of the tub jets when I feel a shift like an electric shock coming from you, igniting my body with desire. My lips find yours and it is every kiss we've ever had or will have, it is a million apologies and regrets. It is us.

"I've never made love in a hot tub before," I say later as we stand together in the steamy shower. "I'm glad there are still some firsts to experience."

You smile at me and begin to massage shampoo into my hair. "Let me know how I can help with those."

I lean back against your chest, losing myself in the feel of your fingers on my scalp and the heat of the water.

It's the little things I find I miss the most. The way you bite your lip when you're concentrating, the sound of your laugh, the way you look at me like I'm the only woman on Earth. These things remind me that we are, at our cores, the same people we once were. We talk about the things that have shaped us since, what fires have wrought these current versions of ourselves. It occurs to me that had we been together for 30+ years I would already know all of these things and not realize there was more to discover. Cancer has taken much from me, but it has given me the ability to appreciate things I might have otherwise missed if I were not counting the number of days left in my life, a true gratitude for the gifts that hide in plain sight. I often look over at you and this warmth suffuses me, softening all of my edges.

This is happy, I think. Finally.

I'm not sure if you're the great love of my life or if I've just built you up to be, but I do know that the feelings I held onto made it impossible for me to be fully present in any other romantic relationship, even my marriage. I didn't allow myself to find happiness where I stood, thinking always that it lived somewhere outside of me, somewhere deep inside your heart. Maybe I still think that, but it no longer matters. I am here and I am happy.

For me, our stories didn't diverge until I'd heard you were getting married. The hope I'd carried for our reconciliation, for you coming back to me, dissipated in that instant. Grief, gray and heavy like a raincloud, enveloped me for longer than I care to admit. It became a part of me as much as the color of my eyes or the shape of my face. It changed me.

It was grieving Grace who met a sweet man with kind eyes and gentle words who fell in love with her almost at first sight. It was that Grace who finally let go of your hand and took the one offered to her and began to look to the future without you.

But the clouds refused to part completely. I was content with him, to a point. Because he wasn't you, could never be you. I tried not to want him to be, tried to love him for it, but I wanted a love like I'd had with you and that was only possible with you. Eventually he found someone who loved him the way he deserved to be loved—he found his happiness while I endlessly searched for mine. I wanted something that wasn't on offer and held an essential piece of myself apart in anticipation of it.

"A WEEK IS not enough," you say as you rub my feet. We're laying on the couch, our legs entwined. The credits on *Roxanne*, an old favorite, have just started to roll, and I've closed my eyes savoring the sweetness of the story, the memories it brought up, and the nearly erotic feel of your strong hands kneading my soles. Tomorrow we leave and go back to our separate lives.

"No, it's not." My eyes stay shut and for once I'm not wondering what you are trying to say, I'm just waiting for you to say it.

"I want you to live with me."

"What?" I ask, one eye open.

"This isn't enough. I want us to live together until..."

"Until I'm dead?" I've abandoned any pretense that the timer on my life is not running out. I'm saying the words now, no matter how much they terrify me.

The pained expression on your face tells me you have yet to land on acceptance, but you nod because you can't pretend.

"You want to take care of me?"

"I want to love you, whatever that needs to look like."

I sit up. "Spoiler alert: you're going to lose me in the end. Can you survive another loss?"

You look at me with such tenderness I almost can't stand it. "I'm going to lose you anyway, aren't I?"

I nod.

"I want more time. We've never had enough time."

"No one does, do they?"

"I want as much as I can get."

"Yeah."

The next morning we move slowly, unwilling to leave this cocoon we've been existing in for the past seven days, unwilling to let anyone else in. Dreading telling our kids what we're planning because they couldn't possibly understand.

"Can't we just stay here?" I say, sitting heavily on the bed. The fatigue I'd not missed has returned, possibly reignited by the weight of the decision I've made, one that I'm sure no one else will understand. It's not even that I care; I just don't want to have to keep explaining myself.

You don't say anything, having learned long ago that I ask questions that I already know the answer to. The bed sags as you sit next to me and gather me into your arms.

"Can we steal that soap?" I ask, smelling your neck for the eleventh time.

"Already done."

"Is there anything that's not done? Do we need to wash the sheets? Clean the place?"

You laugh, but it's a rueful one. Neither of us want to leave but know we can't stay.

The amount of mental energy it requires to will myself up and into the car leaves me spent. On the return trip there are no playlists or spaces to fill with small talk. We sit in comfortable silence while I hold your hand in my lap and doze. I am awakened by your fingers grazing my face.

"We're here," you say.

"We are," I say.

Acknowledgements

Writing, for the most part, is a solitary pursuit; putting a book out into the world is not. I am grateful to have people in my corner who help me to do what I do with joy and enthusiasm and help me to produce something that I am proud to send out into the world.

A big thank you to those who took the time to read drafts of these stories, sometimes more than once: Sophia Lansky, Doug Stevenson, Grace Rose, Donnamarie McGaw, Jennifer Patricia Williams, Kathryn Terry, Susan Stark Ginn, Chloe Adel, Bud Buckley, Andrew Riddle, Kelly Lane Panick, Leslie Merrick, Lola Coryn, Van Kapeghian, and Judith Collins.

A debt of gratitude to my fellow writers at the Florida Atlantic University community writing workshop—your input and encouragement were invaluable. A special thanks to Jamie White for his guidance and insight.

To my wonderful editor, Wayne South Smith, thank you for you helping make this book better than it could have been otherwise. And thank you to author Heather Scarboro Dobson for recommending Wayne.

Megan McCullough, thank you for taking a nebulous idea and making sense of it to create a beautiful cover. It was exactly what it should be.

Some of these stories were previously published, and I am forever grateful to *The Flexible Persona*, *Thrice Fiction*, *Not Your Mother's Breast Milk*, *Red Fez*, and *Drunk Monkeys* for turning my "year of 50 rejections" into a year with none.

And the biggest thank you to Mitch, who makes all of this possible for me. Your support is everything, always.

Connect with Megan

megangordonwriting.com
facebook.com/megangordonauthor
instagram.com/msmegang
twitter.com/msmegan

CPSIA information can be obtained
at www.ICGtesting.com
Printed in the USA
BVHW061937310821
615691BV00016BA/582

9 780986 280252